Land of Misfit Teens

Land of Misfit Teens
Silver Lining Book One

Katie Charles

Praise for Land of Misfit Teens

"I'm not sure what impressed me more: the strong message of this book to stay true to yourself told in a way that wasn't in your face, or the fact the writer was eighteen years old when she wrote it."

Reader, 5 Stars

"This is an amazing book that perfectly captures the teenage condition. The characters are highly believable with all the insecurities and angst that is a reality of the high school experience. I read the book straight through and couldn't put it down."

Reader, 5 Stars

"The author has a real feel for plot and pacing, and the book rolls along at a good clip...Kudos to the author, who manages to convey her message about teen violence without descending into either melodrama or preachiness. If you're a teen, the parent of a teen, or, yes, were a teen, you won't want to miss this fine book."

LAS Reviews, 4 Stars

Art
REQUIRES HEART
#SupportArtistsNotAI
www.GailDelaney.com

TO MY GRANDFATHER, PAPA SHOES.
AKA HAMMERIN' HANK HUGHES

YOU DIED BEFORE I FINISHED THIS BOOK. I WANT YOU TO KNOW I LOVE YOU AND I ALWAYS WILL.

YOU WILL ALWAYS BE PART OF MY LIFE. YOU USED TO TELL ME YOU BRAGGED ABOUT MOM AND ME EVERYWHERE YOU WENT. YOU WERE ALWAYS SO PROUD OF US. YOU ENCOURAGED ME TO THINK ON MY OWN WHEN IT CAME TO CONTROVERSIAL TOPICS, AND NOW I HAVE A TRAIT I HAVE BEEN PRAISED FOR BECAUSE OF YOU.

THIS BOOK GOES TO YOU BECAUSE EVEN IN THE HARDEST TIMES YOU WERE THERE TO HELP. YOU ALWAYS SAID YOU WERE PROUD OF ME. I JUST WISH I HAD HAD A CHANCE TO TELL YOU HOW PROUD OF YOU I AM. YOU FOUGHT IN VIETNAM, PLAYED MUSIC WITH SOME OF THE BEST, AND DIED DOING SOMETHING YOU LOVED.

THAT WOULD MAKE ANYONE PROUD.

To Victoria Arlen.

You are my role model. We have both been between a rock and a hard place and we looked at it two different ways. I felt crippled and ashamed because of what happened to my leg. But when I talk to you, I see how you see yourself.

You are confident, proud, and just plain amazing. The world needs a lot more people like you. I am glad I lived in front of your house for all those years growing up, and I wish we had gotten to know each other better.

I hope this book shows how much I look up to you.

Always stay strong and keep doing what you are doing. You have shown me how strong a person can be. Just know that I will always remember you for the strong beautiful person you are. And I hope the Victoria in this book does you justice.

Book Content Expectations

Topics in this book include terminal illness, the death of a parent, job loss, displacement, moving, bullying, School violence, school shootings, gun violence, the death of a friend, and living in poverty

The high school is fictitious and intentionally not named. Any school – universities included – specifically part of the storyline are also fictitious.

The Silver Lining Series

A young adult & new adult series about staying true to yourself.

Book One: Land of Misfit Teens

Book Two: Picture Perfect

Book Three: The Hand You're Dealt

Prologue

Her dad lost his job.

That should have been the worst thing to happen.

If only...

Amelia's mom was dying.

They'd known for months, but knowing the future never made the pain go away. Knowing death was around the corner made her want to hang on to her mom all the more. Every time she went in her mother's room, she curled up in the small space beside her mother, pretending she was five again and everything was exactly the way it was supposed to be. She read aloud from her mother's favorite books, talked to her about her classes, and the craziness of starting her senior year. Sometimes Mom smiled, sometimes she squeezed Amelia's hand, but mostly she remained still.

Da never spoke of the university or losing his job when he was in Mom's room. He never said it, but Amelia knew he didn't want her to know. It was better this way.

Da had taught there for years, right in the school where he and Mom met. Amelia always planned to go there herself, to finally sit in her father's classroom. She had learned from her parents so much more than any classroom she'd been in, and she didn't have to think hard about why Da was voted Coolest Professor for seven of the last 10 years, but it would have been amazing to sit in a chair in his classroom.

But now, that would never happen. The entire university closed, students and faculty scrambling for new schools to transfer to or to teach at. But, they couldn't leave. Not yet.

Not until...

The cancer was in her mother's heart, which Amelia found painfully ironic since her mom loved her and her dad so much. It hadn't started there, but it was there now, and slowly squeezing her heart to death. Just like everything else, they'd faced down her diagnosis with a unified front. Nothing took down a MacDonald. They'd do this together, just like they did everything. They'd beat it.

Then she'd collapsed when walking away from the dinner table. Amelia called 911 while her father held her mother, calling her name. That may have been just two weeks ago, but it felt like a lifetime ago. Or a blink. Amelia didn't know what time was anymore. A day an hour, it all hurt, and her mother was dying.

She'd never come home again.

They'd never have dinner again.

Her mother would never braid her hair again.

They'd never do anything together again.

Amelia sat in the hall outside her mom's room, the smell of antiseptic and latex making her nose twitch. She had her head on her knees and her hands entangled in her long brown hair. The doctor had come in, his eyes cold, and told her father she should step outside. She'd kissed Mom's cheek and slid off the bed, a heavy lump of dread sitting in her stomach. It made her feel sick and lightheaded.

Her mom was bone thin. Amelia could count her ribs. In two weeks she'd wasted away to a shell of who she had been. When she woke up at all, she looked like a zombie. Amelia hated how her mom already looked dead. Maybe it was supposed to help her accept reality, however horrible it was. Accepting something she didn't like was never her strong point. Da always said not always taking what was handed to her was a strong trait to have. She should never let go of her willpower. Her mother never did. She wanted to believe that she still did. That she was in there demanding to see another doctor, have some more meds, try something different. Not asking but demanding, because that was how her mother worked.

She had that much willpower.

She wouldn't just give up. Would she? Did she have a choice anymore?

What would it take for someone to give up?

If you gave up, was it a form of suicide? Or was there a point when you were allowed to give up? When you know if you try to get better you would only get worse?

Amelia sucked in a hard sob. Her brain wouldn't give her peace, churning and tumbling and making her think things she didn't want to think. Making her accept things she didn't want to accept. She felt cold...hollow...like something was gone.

Something slipped away, leaving her empty.

Amelia heard her dad's familiar steps coming down the hall toward her. She knew it was him. He walked heavy, not like he was stomping, more like his feet were too long for his body and they hit the ground sort of heavy. His brown loafers slipped into the edge of her vision and stopped, then he pulled a chair around to face her and sat down.

She knew. She just knew.

The chair squeaked as he sat.

It couldn't have been goodbye. That kiss on her cheek and squeeze of her hand. That couldn't have been Amelia's goodbye. It just couldn't.

"Amelia..." He pulled her hands down, wrapping his long fingers around hers. She couldn't look up, squeezing her eyes so tight they hurt. She wished she could do the same with her tears. "Sweetheart, Mum is gone." His voice wavered, cracking with each word.

Her chest hurt. She held on tight to his hands, sucking in hard, painful breaths.

Da kissed her hair, laying his cheek against the top of her head. His whole body shook.

Amelia knew that he was trying to be strong. As much as her mom was the fighter, the defender of the family, her father was the strong one when things were tough. That was just how he worked. Mom always said it was the Scot in him. Stay strong for the "lass."

The sound of her mother's voice whispering in her memories made her tremble. She couldn't breathe.

Amelia wept, pulling at Da's sweater until he slipped into the chair beside her and held her against his chest. He held on so tight she couldn't move, but she didn't want to. She and her dad were alone.

Five words took half her world away. She lived for her family. Her mom and dad. Now half of it was gone. Her dad's big hand rubbed her back and he kissed her head. His breath shuttered against her hair.

Amelia's mom was Jewish. The funeral would be quick. Three days at most. No flowers. The Jewish faith didn't kill the living to honor the dead. She and Da would honor her mother and make all the arrangements the way her mother would have wanted.

It was done. Her mother was gone.

New tears ran down everyone's faces. Just when Amelia thought she'd cried herself dry, more tears came and surprised her.

She moved through the ceremony in a daze, her hand firmly in her father's, moving through a crowd of nameless faces and hollow condolences. Everyone meant well, but none of them could understand. Never understand. Finally, it was over.

Amelia got in the car and waited for her dad to say his final thanks to the few remaining guests from the funeral, then they would be on their way. Her mother had no close family to present *Seudat Hawra'ah*, or the Jewish meal of condolence, and her father's family was pretty much all in Scotland. They couldn't make it in time for the funeral, and Da had told them not to take on the expense. Neither she or her father were up to putting on strong faces for his former colleagues and her friends and their families, so they'd asked for everyone to leave them alone once the funeral was done.

Beginning tonight, it would be just her and Da.

She looked at herself in the car mirror while she fingered the black *K'riah* ribbon pinned over her heart, indicating her mother's faith that Amelia mourned a parent. Gray eyes stared back at her. Bloodshot eyes brimming again with tears. Just when she thought she had it under control...

She promised her mom she would stay strong. Last night lying in bed, she promised she'd be strong. A new habit she picked up was talking to her mom all the time, like she was always right there. She had so many things to think about, things she was supposed to figure out with Mom and Da.

College.

How was she going to pull that one off?

She worried she wouldn't be able to go. She had always assumed she'd go to the university her father taught at, but that was no longer possible. Now what? She would never tell her father how much she worried. He would feel so guilty.

Besides, he knew.

She knew he knew.

They'd figure it out. They'd figure out something.

The voices in the surrounding parking lot mingled then went silent and the echo of car doors signaled everyone's departure. Her dad came around the front of the car and got in with Amelia. Shutting the door, he looked at her with a sad glimmer in his dark eyes. She smiled and buckled up. He opened his mouth to say something, but halted mid-breath when his phone rang, blasting the

Batman theme song. He sighed, offered her a crooked grin, and answered it.

Amelia looked her dad over, worried because she knew he hadn't been sleeping much — she'd heard him pacing in the living room. He'd only eaten when she made him. He didn't look too bad for being up for the past few nights. His crazy hair still looked just a crazy as normal. Her mom would have tried to smooth it down, chuckling at the futility of it, but Amelia knew her father didn't care at this point. People always told her she looked like her father. She could believe that. She got her eyes from Mom, but other than that she looked like her Da.

"Liam MacDonald." He paused, his eyes widening and he looked at Amelia, the hint of a true grin making him flash his teeth. "Absolutely! When do you want me? A week? I can do that. See you in a week." He hung up the phone. "Amelia, I just got a job."

Amelia smiled. The first real smile in a week. "That is great, Da! Where?"

"Twenty minutes north by northwest."

"Isn't that a movie?"

"Classic."

"Okay, so…"

"New York, New York," he sang as he turned the key in the ignition. "A wonderful town. The Bronx is up and the Battery' down."

Chapter One

"ABSENCE FROM THOSE WE LOVE IS SELF FROM SELF — A DEADLY BANISHMENT."
~ WILLIAM SHAKESPEARE

LOCKERS SLAMMED IN THE HALLWAY, ECHOING OFF THE HIGH WALLS and ceiling as Amelia MacDonald walked, holding her messenger bag to her chest. She wandered the halls looking for the office where she could get her class schedule.

She was definitely lost.

Down the hall and to the left. Right! She stopped walking and looked at the sign on the wall. Bathrooms to the right, guidance offices to the left, main office straight. Nothing about the registrar's office. Amelia frowned at the wall. She turned around and looked at all the students talking to each other.

Well, someone must know where the office was.

Kids walked past her like she wasn't there, or diverted around like she was a boulder in a stream. She tucked in her shoulders, scanning faces for someone who might help. Three kids came toward her, never visibly acknowledging her. The one nearest her as they past slammed his shoulder against hers and she stumbled, nearly falling and nearly dropping her bag.

He stared back at her, his expression flat. He looked too old to be a student and too young to be faculty. Long hair hung over his forehead, pushed flat by a baseball cap and covering his eyes. Amelia almost said something snarky, but something in his eyes made her stay quiet. Her pulse jumped into her throat and she was suddenly cold. He turned away from her, barely missing a beat.

Amelia blinked, shifting her bag in her hold.

"Ignore him," a girl's voice said in her peripheral, making her jump. She turned her head to look at the speaker. The girl was slightly taller than Amelia, with dark blond hair pulled in a pony-tail. "Most of us do."

"Do what?"

"Ignore him," she repeated and smiled. "He's creepy at best, crazy at worst. And you look lost."

Amelia huffed. "I am."

"I've seen the look before. What are you looking for?"

"Registrar's office."

"You probably need the guidance office," she said, pointing at the signs on the wall. "Go left."

"Thank you."

The bell rang, immediately followed by the synchronized slamming of lockers and her savior disappeared in the crowd before she could ask her name. Amelia pressed herself against the wall so everyone could get by and she could avoid getting trampled by the onset of kids potentially late for class. Things might be easier to find with everyone gone. The hallway quickly cleared out, doors slamming closed all along the hallway. Holding her bag in one hand at her side, she followed the signs to the guidance offices.

Amelia pushed the door open and looked at the secretary behind the front desk. She smiled and walked in.

"Hi, my name is Amelia MacDonald. I'm new here and honestly, completely lost," she said. "Can you tell me where the registrar's office is so I can get my class schedule and books?"

The woman stood up. She was an older woman, bone thin, with skin that looked liked crumpled onionskin parchment. "Are you already enrolled?" she asked, her tone flat and dull.

"Yes, ma'am. We did that last week. They told me to go to the registrar's office today."

"It's not here," she said, walking away from the desk to pull something off the printer. "If you're already enrolled, see the registrar."

"Yes, ma'am," Amelia said, trying to cool the tone she felt threatening. "I need to get my class schedule," Amelia interjected as gently as she could.

The woman sat down. "Like I said, not here."

Amelia stared, blinked, and sighed.

"Thank you, ma'am."

She grabbed her bag and went back to the empty hall, rubbing her temples. She was still lost. Not looking where she was going, she rounded a corner and ran right into someone. She dropped her bag with a grunt, and nearly fell down, but her Da grabbed her arms.

"Oh, I am so sorry for that, Amelia. You a'right?"

"Da, thank God it's you. I am so *lost* in this place and the secretary in the guidance office was no help at all."

"Okay, okay. Do you have your classes yet?" he asked. He took off his glasses and cleaned them with the overcoat to his suit.

"No, not yet. That's how I got lost."

"Well, you could have texted me or something. I know where the office is." He grinned, ridiculously proud of the fact.

"Aren't you supposed to be teaching a class, Da?" she said poking fun and trying not to laugh at his comically proud smirk.

"No, my first period is open. Now, *next* period is a different story," he said with a wink and a click of his cheek.

Amelia rolled her eyes.

"Well, if that is the case, where's the registrar's office?" Her dad grabbed hold of her shoulders, turned her around, and pointed to an unmarked door. "Well, fine. What is it doing as an unmarked door?"

"Don't know," he said with a shrug. "I guess they figure the kids here know where it is. Although..." He pulled his lips back from his teeth in a grimace and ruffled the hair near his neck. "I get the distinct impression the goal of this place is to get kids in and out, and that's about it. Bare minimum. My expected curriculum is pathetic."

"Says the guy with a doctorate in English literature."

"Everyone has to start somewhere. I'm hoping my interpretation of the requirements might be flexible. It lacks encouragement for a secondary education."

"That's horrible," Amelia said. "Mom would have killed me if I ever even thought about not going to college."

"Hey, I'm the former university professor here," Da said, jabbing a long finger at his own chest. Amelia turned to face her dad, and he turned his pointy finger on her. "I may be a high school English teacher now, but *you*, young lady, are still going to college."

"Why are those things opposing facts?" I asked, squinting at him. "I plan on going to college, Da, you know that. It's just sad. People should be able to do what they want, not what someone else says."

"You sound just like her." Amelia looked up at her father, her throat catching at the sad glint in his eyes. "Been reading your mother's journal again." He said it as a statement, not as a question. She nodded, not surprised by the tightening of her throat. He sighed. "I know. I have, too."

Amelia smiled and took her dad's hand. They stood silent, remembering. Another teacher walked passed them and cleared her voice, giving them an odd look. Amelia's dad straightened and brushed off his jacket. "I have to go finish setting up the room. Go on with you now. Get your classes."

"Yes, Da."

"Hey, it's Professor MacDonald here," he said with a wag of his finger, but his smile immediately softened. "I love you, and remember, *behave*." He smiled and turned around on the balls of his feet, his jacket flaring.

Amelia smiled. Her dad was weird, but a lovable weird. And he was her Da. She turned around and went into the register office.

Inside was a woman at least somewhat younger than the last lady Amelia asked for help. She had too much makeup on and looked like she didn't know it was no longer the Eighties. Bubble gum, big hair, blue eye shadow, and all. The office air held a tingle of aerosol smell and some kind of smell like baby powder.

"Hello, my name is Amelia MacDonald. I was told to come here to get my classes."

The woman stared at her and popped a bubble with the gum.

"Who told you that?"

Amelia fought the urge to bang her head against a wall. Instead she looked around the woman's desk; she had a name tag unlike the person in the guidance office. "A woman in the guidance office said I needed to find the registrar since I'm already registered. Ms. Copper, may you please print out my schedule so I may attend class?" The woman looked at her and began typing on the computer. "May I also have a map of the school so I know where I am going?"

Ms. Copper stopped typing. "Well, you just want everything."

"People say that about me," Amelia responded.

The woman rolled her eyes and went on typing. "M-C-D-O-N—"

"Mac, actually," Amelia interrupted. "We're Scottish, not Irish."

The woman stared at her long enough it actually made Amelia feel weird, then went back to typing. "M-A- C-D-O-N-A-L-D."

"Yes, ma'am."

The printer behind Amelia started cranking out paper.

"It's all there," Ms. Copper said with a wave of her hand, flashing neon pink fingernails. She didn't even bother to get up from her desk. "You'll get your books from each teacher. Some forms need to be signed by a parent or guardian. Just saying you're supposed to be here and plan on graduating."

"Yes, ma'am, you will have these tomorrow."

"Whatever." The woman popped her gum.

Amelia nodded.

"Like I said, you'll have them by tomorrow." The woman grunted in response and Amelia left the room. She stood in the hallway and sorted through her papers and put the one she didn't need in her bag.

"Mom, help me. I don't think I'll like this school," she muttered. Amelia looked at the paper that had her classes on it. Advanced Math first. "Look, Mom, Advanced Math. You used to teach that. Easy Peasy, right?" Picking up her bag, she followed the map until she found the right room.

"Well, here I go," she whispered. She opened the door to a bunch of screaming students. The teacher was writing on the board ignoring the paper balls flying through the air. One girl dressed in blue saw her and nudged the girl next to her. It was a quick ripple effect and everyone stopped talking. She stepped inside the door and the whole class stared at her. The teacher turned and looked.

"Can I help you?" he asked.

"Um, yeah. I'm Amelia MacDonald. I'm new and I'm in your class."

The teacher nodded and Amelia stood in the doorway looking at the students. The silence was broken by someone coughing. Oh yeah, this was going to be fun.

Chapter Two

"ALL THE WORLD'S A STAGE, AND ALL THE MEN AND WOMEN MERELY
ACTORS; THEY HAVE THEIR EXITS AND THEIR ENTRANCES; AND ONE MAN IN
HIS TIME PLAYS MANY PARTS, HIS ACT BEING SEVEN AGES."
~ WILLIAM SHAKESPEARE, *As You Like It*

"DID YOU HEAR WE GOT A NEW GIRL? " JOAQUIN ASKED OUT LOUD. HE reached into his locker and put a Yankees cap down over his dark forehead. "Who changes schools two months into her senior year? She's probably trouble," he scoffed.

"Dude, we don't even know who she is yet," Darius said, shaking his head. "How do you even know she's a senior?"

"I heard stuff." Joaquin shut his locker and looked at him. "Five bucks says she's trouble."

"You are so on," Darius said.

"Hey guys, have you heard about the new girl?" Victoria asked as she and Jakkie reached them.

"Who *hasn't* heard about the new girl?" Darius responded. "Joaquin and I were just discussin' her."

"I saw her this morning," Jakkie said. "She looked lost and Creepy Carl practically knocked her down. I told her to go to guidance. Why would someone switch schools at the beginning of the year? She looks like she's probably a senior"

"See? Told you she's a senior," Darius said, jabbing a finger at Joaquin.

"Maybe she *isn't* a senior," Victoria proposed. "Might not be her senior year."

"I don't care whose it is, senior year is senior year," Jakkie said.

"That makes no sense," Victoria said, pulling a face. "Your blond is showing, Jakks."

"Maybe not to you, but it does to me, Red," Jakkie argued. If Victoria was going to mock her blond hair, she was going to mock Victoria's red hair.

The group went silent. They each opened and closed their lockers getting ready for class.

"Has anyone seen Drake or Andrew?" Victoria asked.

"Not Andrew, but I have class with him next. Drake said he was going to practice," Jakkie replied, leaning against her locker and looking into the crowd of people in the hallway. She opened her mouth to say something but was cut off.

"That's all that boy does. Practice," Victoria said as she slammed shut her locker door.

"He has a way out. Don't give him a hard time for that," Jakkie said. "He's one of the lucky ones."

"I'm not." The bell rang and they all walked to the next class.

"Advanced Mathematics, my butt," Amelia mumbled under her breath as she wandered the halls. "That was Algebra II. I did that freshman year. I should be in Statistics. Now where the crap is my locker?"

The hallway was just about empty. A student here or there but not like the main hallways. "Good thing, Amelia. They see you talking to yourself and you'll really make friends fast."

The hallway felt creepy this empty. She heard the noise of the main hallways but no one was in this part of the school. She looked at the numbers on the lockers. They were getting close to the number on the paper with her classes on it.

"Aha!" she yelled as she found it.

She opened the locker and put her math book in it. She wasn't carrying it around. Heck, even opening it would be unlikely. It wasn't the school's fault she'd tested out of several levels of math. They were just going by standard school guidelines. Mom was a math teacher and Da was an English Lit professor. She was doing math two grade levels higher by the time she hit middle school.

She sighed. "This is going to be a long school year."

Amelia slammed shut the locker door, and in the silence, she caught music drifting in the air. Violin music. Amelia picked up her bag and stood there absorbing the sound. It sounded like something her mother would play in the car, intricate and delicate.

She hitched the bag on her shoulder and walked around the hall, hoping to find the source of the music. The music changed. It was melodic now, but slightly creepy sounding, like some music you would hear in the background of a horror movie. The music got louder as she headed further down the hall. She reached a green door with chipped paint and put her ear against it to hear if it was the room where the music was playing. It was.

The door creaked as she opened it. The person standing in the room paid no attention to her and kept playing, his back to her. Amelia looked around the room. It was a music room, but she wasn't sure it was used very often. Music stands were toppled over and chairs were arranged in a lopsided shape of an arch, like students had left in a hurry. Amelia was never in band, but she had a few friends at her old school who always complained about the conductor letting them out late and they had to rush to class. Maybe that happened everywhere.

Amelia walked around the room, trying not to distract the boy playing. He was good. Really good. She wanted to see who he was. She came around in front of him and stood silent while he played. His eyes were closed. He had what looked like it might have been a short haircut at one time, but needed a trim, so was a little long, and his hair was the same color as hers, brown. His head tilted into the chin pad of the violin.

The only person Amelia had ever really watched play music was her mother when she played the piano. Her mom would just let the music flow out of her, she said. She would feel it. Mom honed Amelia's math skills, and Da had her reading by the time she was four, but no matter how she tried, Amelia never managed to be musical. It just didn't click. She could listen to it, and enjoy it, but not play it. Not like Mom.

The boy standing in front of her felt the music. Just like Mom.

He stopped, finishing the piece. Amelia thought it looked like he was letting the last note rest inside him. Her mom would say that when she finished a song. It was giving respect to the composition. Then he opened his eyes and leaned back, looking confused, like maybe he hadn't noticed she came into the room. Amelia spoke first.

"That was really good. But do you know anything with a little more kick?"

He smiled, a slow grin that made her arms goosebump, and brought the violin back up to his chin, the bow resting on the strings. The silence was killing Amelia. What was he going to do?

With a jerk that made Amelia start, he launched into the melody line to "The Devil Went Down to Georgia," a song she always figured needed a fiddle, not a fancy violin. Amelia grinned. Violin, fiddle...whatever it was, this guy could *play*.

He wasn't super tall, but could easily reach things up high if need be. He had bright green eyes. He was kinda cute, and definitely knew what he was doing. By the time he hit the final pulls of the song, his hair fell across his forehead from rocking his head back and forth with each draw of the bow and Amelia found herself bouncing on her toes from the fast beat. With a flourish, he drew out the last note and dropped both his bow and violin to his sides.

"Enough kick for you?" he asked, his breathing short, a wide grin on his face.

Amelia nodded and stepped onto the riser to reach him.

"You are *very* good." She stuck out her hand. "I'm Amelia. MacDonald."

He chuckled and switched his bow into the same hand holding the violin, wrapping his fingers around both the bow and the instrument neck. He shook her hand.

"Drake Casey, and thank you. Being good is my goal. I have to put this away before the bell rings for class," he said, holding up the violin and bow. She nodded, taking back her hand. "Are you the new girl everyone is talking about?" he asked over his shoulder as he crouched over the case.

Amelia laughed a little bit, but felt warmth rush to her face.

"Well, I'm new, but I don't know why everyone would be talking about me. I haven't done anything yet."

"Yet?" he asked, closing the case.

"Yep, 'yet'. I like to make an impression," she said, shrugging her shoulders.

"You managed that much. Do you need help getting anywhere? To your next class maybe?"

"Yeah, that would be great." She held back the urge to yell "Yes!" and punch the air. She had been wandering around this school like a lost puppy. "Do you know where Mrs. Jones' English class is?"

"Yeah, I have her first period." He walked to the door and held it open for her. She nodded and followed him out of the room.

"First period I have *Advanced Mathematics*." She used air quotes. "With what's his face."

"Mr. Quam. I have him, too, but at the end of the day. Not impressed by the class?"

She shrugged. "Not really. My mom teaches math so I'm a little more advanced than advanced math." Amelia realized she'd spoken about Mom in the present tense, but immediately pushed the thought aside. *Not right now*. She stopped walking. "Do I sound like a snob?"

"Nah. I have a Calculus book under my bed I study from at night."

"Just some light reading?" she said with a smirk.

He grinned back and chuckled, then used the violin case to point toward a door. "There's your English class."

"Thank you," Amelia said.

"No problem. If you need any more help, you can find me in the music room most of the time."

"What about lunch?"

"I'll be in the lunch room. You can join my friends and me if you want," he said.

Amelia nodded. "That would be great. Meet back here at lunch hour?"

Drake nodded and walked away. Amelia watched him go and merge into the crowd. The bell rang and everyone started to go on to his or her next class. She walked into the room where she was to have English class. She would have much rather have English in the class her father was teaching, and she supposed she understood why they put her in the class they did, she just didn't have to like it. It would have been her chance to finally sit as a student in his classroom.

"Hello, Mrs. Jones," she said as she walked in to the room. A few students who had already entered the class looked up at her. The teacher was a young teacher maybe in her thirties.

"Hello, and you are?" she responded.

"Amelia MacDonald." She walked up to the desk. "I'm new." She pulled the schedule out of her pants pocket and showed it to the teacher. Students started to whisper to each other. The teacher looked at it.

"Welcome, Amelia. Your seat is in the row by the window and third seat back. I will give you the reading material we have been working on in a moment."

Amelia nodded.

As she turned to take her seat the teacher spoke again. "Are you related to Professor MacDonald?"

"Yes, I am. He's my Da." Amelia smiled. "I mean, my dad." She had to remember most people didn't *get* the whole Scottish thing.

The teacher nodded. "Right, I can see how you look like him. Please take your seat."

"Yes, ma'am." Amelia sat down and looked out the window. A deep ache settled into her chest

Since they'd arrived in the city, they'd been busy. Moving into the only apartment they could find with short notice, getting things set up, and Da had to work out the details of his new employment. Since that morning, she had been shuffling through her new moves. That moment was the first she had to take a breath.

And her chest ached.

Chapter Three

"Good morning, students. I am Professor MacDonald. I am the new permanent teacher. No more long-term subs for you. Nope, you will spend the rest of English this year with me." He walked around his desk and leaned against the desk with his ankles and arms crossed. "Any questions?"

"What's your accent?" a voice rang out.

"Yeah, where you from?"

"Scottish," he answered sitting on the desk, not leaning on it like most teachers. "Thus, the obvious next answer is Scotland. Four score and however many years ago, or something like that — not really, it was about twenty-five years ago — but that is far beside the point. Let's just say I don't take no MC because I am a Mac." He paused. There was no response from the room as students exchanged glances. "No? No one gets it. Mac, PC. No? Well, okay then, we can move on."

Jakkie really didn't care what he said. She was here. That's about all she could or would manage. Didn't much matter anyway. She leaned over the arm of her desk and whispered to the boy next to her. "Andrew, where have you been?"

"I had things to do," he whispered back.

"Like what?"

"Just stuff. Can we leave it at that?"

"No," Jakkie responded in a *you should have known the answer* tone. Andrew rolled his eyes, dug his hand in his pocket, and pulled out his phone. He tapped in his security code, opened chat, and read a message.

"It's Drake. He met the new girl. Said she's nice and sitting with us at lunch," Andrew said, texting back. "I told him it was fine, only if she wanted to be an outcast to the rest of the school."

"Does it really bother you that much?" Jakkie asked. He shot her a glare. Jakkie rolled her eyes and huffed. "You know who your friends are, so everyone else can just go to hell. You know we are always here for you."

"Except when guys like Creepy Carl and his friends catch me alone," he hissed back.

Jakkie's eyes widened and her jaw dropped. She took another look at Andrew, and this time she saw the shadow under one eye and the long bruise along his hairline, mostly hidden by his light brown hair. "Is that what happened? Did they beat you up?"

Professor MacDonald cleared his voice. The two teenagers looked away and acted like they were paying attention. Professor MacDonald went back to talking. Jakkie sat back in her chair. Andrew started texting on his phone again. Seconds later her screen lit up with a message.

The new girl's name is Amelia MacDonald.

Jakkie went wide-eyed. "The new girl is the new teacher's daughter," she croaked, struggling to keep her voice at a whisper.

"I guess so," Andrew said with a shrug.

"How desperate is this family?" Jakkie asked more to herself than anything else.

Brook-Hi had to be the worst school in the state. At least that was how it felt to Jakkie. She once heard a kid from another district say they'd rather be homeless than go here. They also went to an arts and humanities school, so they already thought they were better than anyone else. Most kids like that did. Except for Drake. He was different. Brook-Hi went through teachers faster than kids could learn their names.

But this teacher brought his daughter here?

Andrew slapped Jakkie's arm. She glared at him and he pointed at the front of the room. She followed his lead and looked forward. Professor MacDonald now stood on top of his desk. She opened her mouth in shock.

"What the hell does he think he's doing?" she asked.

"This teacher is crazy," Andrew replied.

"I am making a stand," Professor MacDonald yelled. "We need to start a mutiny!" He waved the curriculum reading book over his head. "I am here to feed your minds! Revolution!" He punched his fist in the air. The students stared at him. "Well, the least you could do is agree," he said, shoving his hands into his brown pants pockets. He sounded both offended and put out by their lack of response, and stepped off the desk landing solidly on his feet.

Amelia looked at the book in shock. Seriously? The title said *To Kill a Mockingbird*, but that couldn't be true. She'd read this years ago. She flipped through the pages. Only two-thirds of the words were legible, the rest had been scribbled out or written over with vulgar language. She made a face as she tried to read.

The students were supposed to be reading silently. Voices grew louder as time passed until the teacher stopped caring and everyone was just about yelling to be heard over everyone else. Amelia heard her name a few times but chose to ignore them.

The bell rang. *Salvation!* This school gave her a headache. How could schools barely half an hour apart be so different? She put the mutilated book into her bag and walked out of the room. Her next class was nearby. She had seen it when she walked with Drake from the music room.

Amelia jumped backwards when two people ran around the corner and cut her off, one chasing the other. They ran by so fast she just saw the blur, but she thought maybe the one doing the chasing had been with the guy who'd run into her that morning. She watched them run down the hall and round another corner. The words they were yelling disappeared with them. Threats. Amelia shook her head.

She walked away looking for the door to her next class. When she found it she swung the door open ready to make another loud entrance, make a scene and announce she was the new girl. Instead she heard a girl yell out in pain. Amelia looked behind the door and saw a red-haired girl standing on one foot holding up her other foot.

"Oh my gosh, are you okay?"

The girl nodded, still grimacing. "Yeah, I'm fine. Going to hurt for a little bit. I've had worse happen," she responded, putting her foot down. "Are you in this class?"

"Yeah, this is history right?"

The red-haired girl nodded. "Hey, are you Amelia?"

"That's me," Amelia admitted with a tilt of her head and a shrug.

"Cool! We have an open seating chart, so you should sit next to me. I'm Victoria, by the way." She stuck out her hand.

Amelia took it. "Amelia MacDonald."

"McDonald. What is that, Irish?"

Amelia gasped and feigned insult. "I think not! Mac is Scottish. Mc is Irish."

"Right, I knew that," Victoria replied.

The two girls walked into the room side-by-side. Victoria went to a seat and Amelia went up to the teacher. This teacher was an older man, not crazy old, not nearly as old as the woman in the Guidance Office. But he had some extra weight, and some of those bifocals with the obvious line in them on the tip of his nose. His hair looked thinner at the top of his head but at least he didn't have a comb over. Ick.

"Hello, sir. My name is Amelia. I'm new," she added but realized too late it was a silly statement. Everyone seemed to know she was "the new girl." The man looked up at her from the papers on his desk, squinting over the top of his glasses. "Is there any material I need for this class? A book?"

The man shook his head and tossed his glasses on the desk. His old chair squeaked when he leaned back and stared at her. "No, I'm better than a book," he started. "But it is a little late for a new student."

"It's only the beginning of October," Amelia replied.

The man grunted in reply, sat forward again and put his glasses back on. Amelia took that as him telling her to go find a seat. Victoria waved at her and pointed to the seat next to her. In the back. Amelia smiled. Three people were nice enough to talk to her; maybe there would be hope for this school yet. She just wished she'd gotten the name of the girl who had helped her that morning.

"So you're Scottish?" Victoria asked. Amelia nodded. "You have the same last name as the new teacher." It was more of a statement than a question.

"He's my Da," Amelia replied. Victoria scowled, like she didn't understand. "He's my father," Amelia clarified.

"Really?" Victoria asked. Victoria seemed shocked. She put a hand to her chest and the other hand to her forehead in a dramatic pose worthy of a soap opera. "Makes sense, I mean the two of you look alike."

"Do you have him as a teacher?" Amelia asked.

"No, but Jakkie and Andrew do. Apparently he stood on top of the desk yelling about starting a mutiny. Does he do stuff like that all the time?"

Amelia smiled and nodded. "All the time."

"Seriously? If my dad did stuff like that, I'd be so embarrassed."

Amelia shrugged. "That's just how he is. And if you get into it, it can be fun." Amelia loved Da and loved absolutely every quirky thing about him. He dressed up as a pirate for Halloween every year when he taught at the university and wore a red stocking cap with a jingle bell on the end for two weeks before Christmas. That was just her Da.

"What does your mom do?"

Amelia paused, swallowing hard against the sudden lump in her throat. This time, she chose her words correctly even if they sucked. "She was a high school math teacher, but my mother passed away." She was going to say more but the bell rang for class to start. The old man, Johnson, according to her class schedule, stood up and started writing on the board.

"Oh my God, I'm sorry. What was her name?" Victoria whispered.

"Lily. Her name was — is — Lily MacDonald. And it's fine. I'm not in denial over it or anything. And don't get me wrong, I still love to talk about her," Amelia whispered back. She looked at the front of the room and saw the teacher looking at her. She smiled at the teacher and he went back to talking. A folded peace of paper landed on her desk. Amelia opened it.

How did she die? If you don't mind me asking.

Amelia pulled a pencil out of her bag and wrote back.

She had cancer.

She folded the paper and handed it to Victoria. She read it and put the paper in her bag. Amelia looked at her. "How can you not be sad?" Victoria asked.

"I *am* sad she's gone, but I'm happy she's not dealing with it anymore."

"I like your outlook. You have plans for lunch?"

"Yeah, I do. A guy named Drake said I could sit with him and some of his friends."

Victoria's face lit up. "I have a feeling we will be having lunch together then." Victoria leaned back in her chair smiling

Chapter Four

"How do you like that? Even among misfits, you're a misfit."
~ Yukon Cornelius
Rudolph the Red Nosed Reindeer and the Island of Misfit Toys.

"Our group consists of the people that don't fit in elsewhere, for whatever reason," Victoria explained while they waited outside Mrs. Jones' classroom for Drake. She rolled her eyes and sighed before saying, "We all have names for each other that everyone else decided. Which means we probably don't like them. I'm the Clumsy One. Darius is the Confused One. Drake is the Closet Genius. Joaquin is The Geek. Jakkie is the Super Lucky One. And Andrew is Jiminy Cricket."

"How is he a Disney character? I mean, if I were going to belong to Disney I would want to be..." She paused. She never thought about this before. She was surprised to realize she might actually be stumped. "Pocahontas! From the *second* movie," Amelia nearly yelled, thrusting her finger in the air in triumph. "When she goes to England." Seemed like a good answer. "You know, off to another world, not having a clue what a toilet was — wait that's *Pirates of the Caribbean.*"

Victoria looked at her like she'd grown an extra nose and slowly shook her head. "He is our conscience. He always knows the right thing to do for everyone else. Not so much for himself. He hasn't been in school for a few days, and Jakkie said we probably shouldn't ask him about it." Victoria tilted her head and tapped her chin. "Now I need to know what Disney character I am. Ariel is the only redhead, so I guess I'd have to go with her. But knowing me, I would either drown or think I was drowning." She shrugged.

"Merida has red hair," Amelia pointed out.

"Right! But my luck, I'd shoot someone with my bow and arrow. Drake!" she yelled and banged her fist against the lockers, startling Amelia.

"You don't have to bang," he said, coming up behind them. "Hey, Amelia. How was class?"

"Boring."

"*You* know that. *I* know that. Heck, even *Victoria* knows that. We all suffer through it."

"Hey, you jerk! Don't be mean," Victoria said, pushing Drake's arm.

"You know I'm kidding," Drake said, looking at Victoria out of the corner of his eye.

"*You* know that. *I* know that. I just don't know if the *new girl* knows that!"

"Hey, don't be mean." Amelia laughed.

"What are you shooting for, the Funny One?" Victoria asked, smiling. She started to walk. Drake and Amelia followed her.

"Better than the Clumsy One," Drake chimed in.

"Hey, I wear my title with pride, Mr. Closet Genius." She turned around so fast that her red hair brushed over her face. "Just be glad I don't kick your butt for that sort of comment." She turned back around and walked again.

Amelia assumed they were going to the lunchroom, but they could have been leading her anywhere. The hall was empty, with only a few students taking their time to get to lunch.

"What are you going to do? Trip over me?" Drake asked

"You jerk." Victoria didn't even bother to turn her head.

"Ouch, I felt the burn in that," Amelia said. "Watch your step there, genius, you might get burnt."

"Oh, he always has to watch himself. For a genius, he is not very smart," Victoria spat. She turned around and opened a double door by pressing her back against the handle. "And he has a mouth. Doesn't know when to shut up."

Amelia put her hand on the door and held it open as Drake walked into the room. Amelia followed.

"This is the cafe. Land of nasty stomach-churning...mystery meat." Victoria paused and hung her head. "Sadly, I am not joking about that."

Drake shook his head and walked passed Victoria, heading to a table. Amelia followed. People yelled back and forth at each other and the room was loud with conversations.

The cafeteria was just like every other room in the building. Plain and white. No color, no posters. It just left the walls boring and sad. It all made Amelia sad. They walked to a table with four other people sitting at it, with the girl being the one who had helped her that morning. When the blond looked up, she smiled. They stopped their conversation and looked at Drake, Victoria, and Amelia.

"Guys, this is Amelia—"

"The new girl..." Amelia finished.

Drake grinned and sat down at the table, leaving an empty chair beside him. The three guys stared at her. Amelia looked back and forth at them. She had to speak. Maybe if she spoke then they would start to speak too. She looked to the girl who had helped her.

"Thanks for helping me this morning. Law of Exclusion, since Victoria told me about everyone, you're Jakkie? The Lucky One," Amelia asked, and Jakkie nodded. The guys still said nothing. "So, who's The Geek? The Confused One?" Still nothing. She looked around at the people. "Oh, come on Jiminy, speak to me!" She slammed her hands on the table.

"Is your dad really the new teacher?" Jakkie asked, nearly

jumping when she blurted out the question. Apparently she didn't respond fast enough because a "Well?" was asked by someone else at the table.

Amelia chuckled to herself before answering.

"Yep, that's my Da. Do you have him as a teacher?"

"Yeah, me and Andrew," Jakkie answered, pointing toward a guy with light brown hair and the remnants of a black eye. "He stood on the desk in class." She tilted her head toward another boy at the table. Amelia quickly ran the names through her head. *Jakkie is lucky. Victoria is the redhead and the Clumsy One and Drake is hot — no, Drake is the Closet Genius.*

"Yep, that's Da."

"I thought teachers lived at school and hung from rafters in the ceilings." one boy said.

Ahh so he is The Geek. Had to be Joaquin.

"Only if they're Krillitane," Amelia said with a grin.

"Well, Doctor Who did it, why can't it happen in real life?" The boy smiled. "I like you. Sit down."

"Can you agree the show sucked once David Tennant left?" Amelia asked, squinting. This was a defining moment for her — for them. His answer would determine the worth of the entire group.

"I don't know...I *liked* Matt Smith. Until River Song came and messed it up," he said.

Amelia thought it over. He did have a point. River Song was really the show killer, even when Tennant was around. "Okay, I can accept that." Amelia took the seat next to Drake. "I'm still torn on all the Doctors and changes after that." She focused on the final, unnamed dark-skinned boy. "More Law of Exclusion. You gotta be Darius. The Confused One."

Darius scowled and looked between his friends. "I hate that name. I don't understand why you—"

"And thus why you're called the Confused One," Jakkie teased, bumping her shoulder against his.

Some students walked behind their chairs and an awful, gag-worthy stench hit her and she wrinkled her nose. "What is that *smell*?!"

"I told you. Mystery meat in gravy," Victoria said

"Good thing I brought a bagged lunch."

She pulled a plastic bag out of her backpack and so did everyone else except Darius. Jakkie took a sandwich from her bag and set it on the table in front of him. Darius gave a crooked smile and took the sandwich out of the plastic sandwich bag. Amelia smiled to herself. Oh yeah, they liked each other. It was crystal clear. The group began eating and talking about what they did the night before and the plans for the upcoming weekend.

"So, Mom said I could have some people over this weekend. We could do another horror movie fest," Jakkie said. Everyone agreed. "Amelia, you can come, too. We need another girl around to even out the votes some more."

Amelia thought about how much she needed to unpack and sort out. But her dad did say this morning he wanted her to make friends. "Yeah, I'll be there. I just have to check with Da. To see if he has no plans."

"Wait, Da?" Joaquin asked.

Amelia nodded. "Yep. In Scotland, that's how you say dad. Da. So I call him Da."

"I can understand that," Jakkie said and bit into her lunch. "It's kinda cool," she mumbled around her mouthful of peanut butter and jelly.

There was a pause before Joaquin spoke out again. "Hey, we are seven. Seven is the number of Epic! We are now Epic."

Amelia and a few others nodded their head. They all got it.

I could get used to these people. They understand seven.

Chapter Five

"It was times like these when I thought my father, who hated guns and had never been to any wars, was the bravest man who ever lived."
~Harper Lee, *To Kill a Mockingbird*,

"Amelia, I got the television working!" Da yelled across the apartment. "And we get our channel!"

Amelia came around from a stack of boxes holding a pot.

"Well, turn it up. We can take a break from unpacking for a half hour." She put the pot down on another box and dropped down on the couch propping her feet on the table.

"Feet off," her dad said. She slid her feet off and he dropped onto the couch beside her, slamming his feet on the table, one sneaker at a time. Amelia glared at him. "Yeah, so what?"

"Da, you jerk."

"Fine, put your feet up. As long as I'm no longer a jerk."

"Agreed," Amelia responded and put her feet up beside him. They both had on Converse sneakers, hers purple and his red.

He cranked up the volume and grinned at Amelia like a maniac.

"...or is she just another Bridezilla?" the television roared.

"Can you believe it? She sucks her thumb? How childish," Amelia ranted.

"Your mother never acted like that when we were getting married," he said, leaning closer to her so his shoulder touched hers.

"I can't imagine Mom ever being a bridezilla."

"Hey, she was *not* happy with me on our wedding day."

"Well, yeah, only because Immigration crashed the wedding. I think she had a right not to be happy. I still think it's funny. I wish I could have seen her face."

"No, you did *not* want to see her face." He scowled, his brows pulling down over his eyes as he grimaced. "I was scared..."

"How did you convince them you were legal anyway?"

"There was a reason I always carried my green card on me everywhere we went. And why I got my citizenship shortly after. No need to travel that road again."

They stopped talking when the commercial ended, only to laugh out loud at the antics of the crazy bride-to-be on the television. This was their "thing". If *Bridezillas* was on, they watched it, and did a dance of joy if they discovered a marathon. When the commercial came back on, her father shook his head and handed Amelia an open bag of chips from beside him on the couch.

"I would hate to be that lady's husband. She is just mean."

"I think over half of this stuff is set up for the show, and if not, 'lady' isn't quite the right word, Da. I wonder how much money they get for doing this?"

"If they're getting money for the show, you would think they could afford to pay for the church," her dad responded. He picked some lint off the tee shirt he had changed into after school.

"Maybe it depends on views. Like a royalty check for a book?"

Her dad nodded. "Sure. Makes sense."

The power went out with a snap and a blink. The only sound left in the room was the TV sizzling. Amelia let her eyes adjust to the room. It was dark outside which only made things darker. She got up to go to the window, doing her best not to stub her toes on the stacks of boxes scattered everywhere, and pulled back the shades hoping to let in some light in from the street.

"Amelia, close the shades and step away from the window," her dad whispered. When he whispered, his Scottish accent was thicker than when he was talking normally. When he whispered, and when he was upset. Which didn't happen very often.

"Da? Where are you?"

"Amelia," her dad said again. "Please."

When her father, who tended to ramble on for twenty minutes about anything, answered her with just a couple words, she knew she'd better listen. She let the shade drop back over the window and stepped back. She only tripped once going back to the couch. Her father was still there, and soon as she was beside him, his big hand wrapped around hers, squeezing.

Bang!

Amelia jumped and gasped, her dad's arms wrapping around her. It sounded so near to them. Screams echoed through the apartment. It had to be in the next apartment over. There was another shot and the screaming stopped. Amelia doubled over, put her head on her knees, and covered her head with her arms. She knew what had happened, she just didn't want to believe it. A door slammed and running footsteps echoed from the hall and down the stairs leaving the building. Moments later, an engine roared. They were gone.

Amelia's dad rubbed her shoulders before he stood and went for the phone.

"Landline's dead," he said, setting the phone back in its cradle. Amelia pulled out her cell phone and handed it to her dad. He nodded, his face grim. The beeps of the phone dialing 9-1-1 echoed in the dark apartment.

"Hello, this is Professor Liam MacDonald. There was a shooting in our apartment building and I believe people are hurt." He provided their address.

Amelia raised her head and squinted until she could focus on her father's silhouette against the faint light coming through the street side windows.

"Amelia, sweetheart, find a torch," her father said, turning the phone away from his mouth. Then he straightened and adjusted the phone as if someone had come back on the line. "Yes, ma'am, someone could be badly hurt or possibly dead." He paused, and she held her breath when he hung his head. "No, I didn't see who it was. They ran out of the building immediately."

Amelia stood to rummage around in boxes until she found a flashlight.

Fourteen college books, three piggy banks, and one glass unicorn later she found a flashlight. Actually, she found three flashlights, two of which were dead. Da disconnected the call.

"They're coming to check things out. The operator practically dismissed the call out of hand, but protocol says they have to come down and look around."

Amelia tilted the light to her father. He smiled.

"Well, we could talk about school or how you have been making new friends. Any cute guys? Who knows, you might end up on Bridezilla by school end."

"Da!"

"Oh, fine, I see how it is. Teenage mood swing," he said. Amelia rolled her eyes and threw the flashlight at him. He caught it with ease, grinning wide.

Somewhere from the street below came the sound of sirens. Police. Nothing unusual. Nothing new. Drake slid off his bed, reached underneath and pulled out a large, thick book. Opening to a book-marked page, he reached over to his desk and grabbed paper and a pencil.

"Time to study for my future," he mumbled and groaned. He'd lost precious study time hanging out with the gang.

He knew his violin playing could be a path into college and possible scholarships, and he would leverage the chance as much as possible, but as much as that was his way out he couldn't spend the rest of his life on the violin. He knew better than that. So he studied. Math was the main thing. He knew he would use it everywhere. He had a goal in mind at the beginning of senior year. By Christmas get half way through Stats. That wasn't going so well. He was running out of time. He'd done really well on his SATs and had even taken the ACT to cover his bases, but some schools required a placement test and he wanted to be way ahead of the curve.

He had a hard enough time balancing things: violin, math, school, and lack of parents. He once heard the phrase parented orphan. He had parents, but they were pretty much absent from his life. He hated thinking of it as lack of parents, but that was the truth of it. He lived with them and on the weekends if he woke up early enough, or stayed up late enough, he would see them. Sometimes they were gone because they were working; sometimes they were gone just because they were gone. His mother hated where they were — because of where they had once been — and his father... well, his father would rather drink than face the guilt even though Drake never blamed him. Not for that. Not for losing everything.

It was all the things after that.

So, he did the college application thing. He researched for scholarships. He worked hard. He kept focused because that was the only way out.

And then *she* came into town. He found himself thinking about her. Wondering things he never wondered about Victoria or Jakkie. What's her favorite food? Why are her eyes gray? Victoria told him Amelia's mom had died, so maybe that was why they moved. But, why here? Out of all the places his father could go to teach, why here?

And mainly, how did she feel about him?

He never cared what people thought about him. There was no point. People could hate you for no reason, or for stupid reasons. Like Andrew. Drake and the others had known for a long time that Andrew was bi, and they didn't care. Why care about something like that? But someone had "outed" him and now idiots made his life miserable whenever they could. He'd seen the bruises today. Andrew had stayed out of school as long as he could, but it wasn't long enough to heal completely. Creepy Carl and his friends had beaten him up. Again.

Victoria said Creepy Carl had practically knocked down Amelia in the hallway. That's all it took to get on his bad side. And his bad side – if the rumors were true – could get you dead. So, on top of everything Drake found himself worrying about Amelia. He got the impression she had no idea about how dangerous people could be. She would just walk up to anyone and ask a question, not knowing asking the wrong person the wrong thing could get you dead.

Drake knew she would find her way into trouble one way or another. It was getting her *out* of the trouble he worried about.

He slammed his book shut.

He was thinking about her again.

He had to stop. He was too distracted. He needed to focus. He needed to get out of here. November was around the corner, which meant college applications had to be in soon.

Not that he could afford college, but that was what the violin was for. He applied to all the schools he could that might appreciate his musical skills. All the state schools, all the semi-private schools. Art schools. Heck, he'd even tried Juilliard, even though it was a long shot. A very long shot.

New York School of Music was looking good. They'd reached out to tell him they had him on the shortlist for a tuition scholarship. There were only a few granted each year, and he had a solid chance.

He was never much of a showoff. Hide away in his corner until it was safe to get up and leave. But when Amelia came in and wanted to hear something faster he showed off. No second thoughts about it. Amelia intrigued him. She had guts and that could be a good or bad thing.

He ran his hand over his face and through his hair. He was in a losing battle and he knew it. He just had to choose what battle he was going to win.

Putting the book back under his bed and the paper and pencil away, he picked up his phone and scrolled through his contacts. It had been a couple of weeks since he'd texted Scott Scotch, his best friend from a past life. At least that's what the "time before here" felt like.

Hey, man. How goes it?

Dude! Awesome! What's up?

Oh, nothing...I'm obsessing over grades and music and this new girl.

Usual stuff. I'm trying to study Calculus but my brain doesn't want to shut off enough. A lot on my mind.

I hear ya. How's the college hunt going?

Meh. I'm applying and waiting to hear back. NYSoM might be a possibility.

You should check out Clarkmore. I just got my acceptance letter. It's nice because it's still in New York so I get in-state tuition. Far enough from home, I'll live on campus but I can go home whenever I want.

Maybe I will. I'm looking at a lot of options.

They texted another fifteen minutes before the conversation found a natural end and they signed off. Drake plugged in his phone to charge and decided to just go to bed. Nothing was sticking in his brain anyway, and it was the weekend. He had time to figure out what the heck to do. About the future. About Amelia MacDonald.

Easy, right?

Chapter Six

"Let's go hand in hand, not one before the other."
~ William Shakespeare, *The Comedy of Errors*

Monday came all too soon. It always did. Drake barely paused walking through the metal detectors in the school entrance, nodded to a couple who nodded first, and walked to his locker. He opened it without really focusing, took stuff out of his bag, and put other things in, his violin case in between his feet. He never took chances with it.

Drake jumped when Joaquin slapped his hand against the locker door, slamming it shut.

"Dude, did you hear about what happened to Amelia and her dad this weekend?"

"No," Drake responded, opening his locker again in hopes of hiding the bristle that shot up his spine. He was quite proud of how well he held back his urge to grab Joaquin by the front of his hoodie and shake the answer out of him. Even with the sudden rush of "Oh, crap" that hit him.

"They called the cops on a shooting." Joaquin slammed the

locker shut again. "Do you know where they live? Who their neighbor is?"

Drake turned and faced him.

"Slam my locker on more time I'll slam you in it," he threatened. It was not a real threat, Joaquin new that, but it got the point across. Joaquin smirked and held up his hands, and Drake opened his locker again. "No, I have no idea where they live."

"Their next door neighbor is – *was* – Creepy Carl's girlfriend. She's dead. I give you one guess who did it."

Drake snapped his full attention to Joaquin. "Did they arrest him?"

"No. News said whoever killed her was gone before the police got there. But come one...her dad called the cops on Creepy Carl!"

"They wouldn't be that stupid."

"Did you *not* see the news? Man, it was on the *news*! Their names and everything. No interview, I mean they were smart about that but still, man, they sent out their own death notice," Joaquin ranted.

"I'm telling you, they can't be that stupid."

Jakkie walked up to the two boys and opened her locker. "Are you talking about Amelia and her dad?" she asked. "Because if you are, I can't believe they did that, even if whoever did it was already gone."

"*Whoever*. Do you think if you don't say it, he won't find you? Like Bloody Mary or Candyman or something? I heard he saw them make the call," Joaquin said.

Jakkie shook her head. "Not according to ABC7, by what I hear. They waited till whoever left and then called. But I also heard a rock was thrown through their window."

"No, I heard on WNYW they said a death threat was taped to their door."

"Think about it, Joaquin. Why would someone tape a death threat to the front of their door? Everyone can see that! They would do something only they can see." Jakkie was nearly yelling.

"Oh yeah, because putting a rock through a window is not noticeable at all!" Joaquin yelled back.

"Will the both of you shut up?"

Jakkie and Joaquin stopped mid-argument and stared at him. Drake huffed and picked up his violin case. "Listen to you two. You *heard*. Did either of you actually *watch* the local news?" When neither answered, he shut his locker and shook his head. "We won't know what happened until we ask her. Or until you have Professor MacDonald in class."

They moved down the hall together, heading without having to discuss it to the main lobby where they could talk for a few minutes before classes began. Joaquin told them more horror stories of working the late shift at the local fast food joint, and the more he talked the more Drake decided he was *never* eating there again, even if Joaquin got him employee prices. Jakkie got another mailbox full of college catalogues.

"I mentioned college to my mother and she laughed in my face," Jakkie said. "I mean, I can do community college if I live at home and get a job to pay for it. They're not going to help. Can't."

"Face it, none of our parents make enough money to even give college a thought, and none of us are good enough to get scholarships." He looked sideways at Drake. "Well, most of us. And if our parents *do* have the money, they're—"

"Don't even say it out loud, Joaquin," Drake said, cutting him off.

Amelia walked up to the group before Drake could offer a response. "Hey, what's up?"

"What happened this weekend?" Drake blurted, wrapping his hand around her wrist before he could even think not to.

"Ahh, a question for a question. I can play this game. Umm... why is the gravitational pull the Earth has on the moon so strong?" she asked with a grin.

Drake stared at her, clenching his jaw to keep from saying too much. He let go of her wrist and picked up his violin and backpack.

"Your turn," she said.

"That's not what I'm talking about."

"Oh, that's not a question." She poked his arm. "You started the game, not me."

"You called the cops this weekend." He swatted her hand away.

"Oh, now you see *that* is an assumption. Not a question." She poked his arm again. He moved away but she followed him, still poking his arm. "Da called the cops. There was a shooting in the apartment next to us. What were we supposed to do?"

"Nothing. That's what you're supposed to do," Joaquin answered.

"Did they put a rock through your window?" Jakkie asked

"Did they leave a death threat taped to your front door?" Joaquin asked

"No, and no. Where did you get that idea?" Amelia asked.

She kept poking Drake's arm, giggling each time he pushed her hand away.

"News," the two of them said together.

"You're going to leave a bruise," Drake said, pushing her hand away again.

"Then you will remember me."

"Like I could forget you," he said too quickly. Her finger paused mid-poke and she stared at him. Drake cleared his throat. "You said you wanted to make an impression. I guess you have."

Amelia frowned. "I need a better reason to go down in history than that." She paused. "I'll have to think about that. It has to be big and fun."

Drake shook his head.

"Are you going to tell us what happened?" Jakkie asked.

"What's there to tell?"

"What happened?" Jakkie yelled. She lunged forward, grabbed Amelia's shoulders, and put her face nose to nose to hers. "Tell me woman, or so help me—"

"You'll do what?" Amelia egged her on.

"You don't want to know."

"I'm sure you heard on the news. I mean, it was hard to miss since they used our names."

"The news told us a note was taped to the door and a rock was thrown through your window," Joaquin added.

"What news do you watch? Turn on CNN once in a while."

Jakkie let go of Amelia, crossed her arms, sighed, squinted her eyes and stared at Amelia. Amelia smiled and stuck her tongue out at her. Jakkie huffed at her. Drake chuckled and shook his head.

"I'm going to go practice," Drake said, then the bell rang. "Or...I could go to first period instead." He sighed.

"I'll explain what happened at lunch," Amelia said as she rushed to organize her bag for the first half of the day.

He knew they could walk together part of the way to her classroom, so he waited while she got her stuff. It gave him a chance to study her without being stupidly obvious. Her hair was different. Drake would normally never notice how Jakkie or Victoria did their hair, but Amelia he noticed. It was pulled up in a bun. Normally she let her hair flow down her back. He liked it. Up or down it was nice. They all said their partings, and "see you at lunch" then headed to first period.

That would never have happened if Amelia weren't here. He would have been in the music room as soon as he got to school. He might have not even seen Joaquin or Jakkie. He was so intrigued by Amelia he missed a time slot to practice.

He knew he was thinking about her far too much. All the way to class he replayed everything she said in his head, like he was saving them for later.

This stupid class. Advanced Math. Amelia scoffed as she doodled on a blank page in her notebook. Flowers and hearts. She had to stop herself from writing Drake's name in one of the hearts. That would be bad if the page fell out of the notebook and then the whole school saw. Just another bad script from one of those teenage dramas.

"Ms. MacDonald, are you going to answer the question or just sit there drawing and not paying attention?"

Amelia looked at the board.

"Three."

"No, as you can clearly see, you skipped a step. The right answer is…" Mrs. Anderson walked to the board and solved the problem. "Three. Well, you may have been right this time, but it won't happen every time."

The teacher was displeased. She spoke slower and her voice dropped down an octave. Like Jakkie, she squinted and stared at Amelia, who was wise enough not to stick her tongue out at her. She may have wanted to but knew better than that.

Unlike Mrs. Anderson, Amelia was very pleased. She just did a quadratic formula question in her head. This was simple math. She did these years ago. Her mother was a math teacher and had Amelia doing her multiplication tables in first grade. It was painful to have to sit through it again. But the chance to prove a teacher wrong always made the day seem better.

Amelia put a tally in the corner of the paper, marking the number of brain cells she knew were dying of atrophy by being in this class.

Chapter Seven

AMELIA WAS RUNNING LATE.

She got turned around again getting to the lunchroom and she had to be shown the way. Now she was weaving in and out of the people to get to her locker.

There was a crowd of six people deep in all directions surrounding her locker and the lockers around hers.

"What's going on?" She tried to push past the wall of people to no avail. Trying again she used her backpack as a shield. "Can I get to my locker, please?"

The person to her right turned to face her and knocked her bag out of hands.

"Your locker is here?" he asked.

Amelia bent over and grabbed her bag. "Yeah, and just because I'm *the new girl* doesn't mean my locker is a showroom for the rest of the school."

The boy stared at her. Amelia couldn't tell if he was surprised or scared. The voices talking around her locker grew quiet and they all turned to look at her.

"What?" she asked.

The all moved out of the way and she saw seven lockers covered with graffiti.

Get nosey and get dead.

Amelia looked at it in shock. She walked up to her locker. The part of the message 'and get' was painted on it. She touched the paint. It was dry.

Drake and Andrew ran up to her.

"Are you okay?" Drake asked wrapping his hand around her arm.

Everyone stared at them. Amelia was really beginning to feel like she was trapped in some faux-reality teen drama television show.

"Move on, people," Andrew shouted, waving everyone away. "Nothing to see."

"How did they know my locker was here?" she asked.

A sick feeling sat in her gut, and she didn't like the way her head felt. Confused. Maybe even a little scared. She took a step closer to Drake. She didn't know why, but it made her feel better.

"Why would someone be after you?" Andrew asked.

Amelia laid her palm against her forehead and shook her head. "Probably because Da called the cops on the murder in the apartment next to us on Friday. But it's not like we knew *who* we called against! We called because we thought someone was hurt."

Andrew's jaw dropped open.

"Don't you watch the news?" she said with full sarcasm volume. "According to Jakkie and Joaquin we were the elevon o'clock top story.

"You need a tv for that. Your dad called the cops?" Andrew asked. He pulled out his phone and started texting. "Okay, follow me." He put his phone away and grabbed hold of Amelia's arm, leading her away.

"Do I have a choice?" she asked.

Andrew shook his head. "Get in the classroom." Andrew said shoving Amelia into the room and motioning for Drake to follow.

Drake looked ticked...maybe. She wasn't sure. He was scowling and he clenched his jaw so hard his cheek jerked. He looked both ways before following them into the classroom.

"Hey," Andrew said, and closed the door behind him.

"Amelia?" a soothing Scottish voice asked and Amelia immediately felt better. Amelia turned around. Her father sat at the desk, reading glasses, on holding a large book in his hands. She hadn't even realized they were outside his classroom. "Mr. Casey. Mr. Tayler. Can I help you with something?"

Amelia walked toward him with a sigh, pushing her hands into her back pockets. "I think we upset someone Friday."

Her dad slid his glasses down his nose so he could look over them at Amelia. "And you know this, how?"

"They said so, on the lockers." She shrugged, tilting her head toward the closed door and bustling hallway beyond. "Andrew and Drake are more worried about it than I am. I mean, what can a bunch of people with spray paint do in a school?"

Andrew shook his head. There were three knocks on the door. Andrew opened it and the rest of the group came in all speaking at once, crowding around Amelia.

"Excuse me," Amelia's dad boomed in his best 'teacher voice' to get everyone to be quiet. "Could we all just settle down and explain to me exactly what's going on?"

"Someone sprayed a warning on some lockers in the hall, Professor MacDonald," Drake said, clearing his throat. "One of them was Amelia's."

Her father scowled, one eyebrow rising higher than the other. "So what did the lockers say exactly?" he asked.

"Get nosey and get dead," Drake answered. He pushed forward through the group to stand beside her again.

"And it was spray painted on," her dad said.

Amelia knew her dad was thinking something through. His nose was all wrinkled at the top and his eyes were all crinkled. He'd taken off his glasses, and now tapped the folded spectacles in the palm of his hand. It was always a sign when he said the painfully obvious, meaning he was running things through his head. Victoria, on the other hand, hadn't figured that out yet.

"No, they wrote it in blood," she snarked.

"You shouldn't have made that call. Now we're all doomed," Darius said.

"How are *we all* doomed?" Amelia asked, crossing her arms. She was getting annoyed at how this was being handled. "Not like it was you."

"Puh-lease! They're already after Andrew and they've threatened--" Joaquin started, but Jakkie elbowed him in the ribs. Amelia and her dad exchanged glances.

"Who are we even *talking* about?" Amelia demanded, but they all stared back, silent. "What? Is this some kind of He Who Should Not Be Named crap?"

"Well, first we need to call the headmaster and let him know there has been a threat on campus," her dad said. He went to the classroom phone on the wall and lifted it from the cradle — the phone had to be at least twenty years old — and dialed the main office.

"I need the headmaster — aaah — Principal Weaver."

As he talked, Jakkie leaned toward Amelia. "Did he really just call Weaver a headmaster?" Jakkie asked.

Victoria shushed her.

Da hung up and came back over to the group.

"He will be sending a cleaning team to clean it up. Other than that there is nothing more they can do. No one was physically hurt that we know of, so there is no reason to call the police. CCTV may or may not be working. Apparently destruction of school property doesn't warrant a visit," he explained with a snap of his jaw together.

"So, what...we all go to class and ignore this?" Amelia asked. "Da, that doesn't seem right."

"I know, Amelia." He laid his hand on her shoulder, and she thought she saw a touch of sadness in his eyes. "But it's the way things are. Now go off and have lunch. We'll talk about it at home," her dad said. Amelia reluctantly walked over to the door and opened it so everyone could get out.

"Mr. Casey, Mr. Tayler," Da called after them.

They stopped at the door, one on each side of Amelia.

"Thank you for looking after my daughter," he said with a small nod. Then he put his glasses back on and went back to his desk.

Amelia scowled as she followed them to the lunchroom.

Amelia plopped down at the table, her arms crossed over her chest. Everyone else sat, already moving on to other topics of discussion. It wasn't the first time lockers had been painted, and in truth, paint was minor compared to some things Drake had seen happen. Like the time someone destroyed the biolab and knocked over the vending machines in the cafe. Everyday stuff.

Drake stood at the end of the table, wondering what he should do next. Should he sit next to her? Should he sit on the other side of the table? He had to be careful. Girls tended to read too much into things, or at least Victoria and Jakkie did. He scowled. What did he care what Jakkie and Victoria thought? He cared what Amelia thought, and he'd be a moron to try and convince himself otherwise. Drake decided to sit next to her.

Her gray eyes shifted to him for just a moment, but she went right back to staring at the scarred tabletop. Drake linked his hands together and watched her. "You really never had to deal with this before, have you?" he asked.

"I'm not stupid, Drake. Or nearly as naïve as everyone thinks I am."

"I never said—"

She sat up, flinging her hand out at him. "Of course you have. Everyone has one way or another. I didn't come from some utopia where nothing bad every happened. We lived like half an hour from here! But someone was hurt and what I *do* know is you don't do nothing." She slung her bag on the table and put her head on it.

Drake sighed. "I didn't call you stupid. Girls—"

"Hey!" Victoria and Jakkie yelled.

Drake rolled his eyes. Amelia's head shot up again, her hands talking as much as she was, flailing around like it would help her argument.

"We don't even *know* who the note was for! Maybe it has nothing to do with Da calling. Maybe it was someone else. Maybe it's not about the lady next door to me," Amelia ranted. "Excuse me. The lady who *used* to be next door to me. She's dead." Her voice wavered and she pressed her lips together in a thin line.

Drake opened his mouth to respond but never got a chance. Amelia kept going, pointing a finger at him. "And don't you start thinking I'm scared, because I am not. I'm not saying I'm going to hunt down whoever did this, but I *won't* let them push me around."

Joaquin spoke up before Amelia could start another rant.

"We're not saying anything like that, Amelia. Drake is a stupid genius. He doesn't know when to shut up. We just know who you might have pissed off, and that's why we're worried."

Amelia looked at him. She shook her head a little and let some of her hair fall in her face. Drake never knew much about girls, but that was never a good sign.

"Wow, Joaquin, that is deep" Jakkie interjected.

Amelia looked at them. Drake saw a look of confusion on Amelia's face. Was it confusion? Or was it more disgust? Disapproval? Either way she was frowning and looking through her hair that had fallen in front of her face. God, why did women have to be so confusing?

"Who?" she asked.

"Who what?" Joaquin asked back.

"Who do you think I pissed off?"

"Creepy Carl," Darius said, then looked around like he was afraid Carl had heard him.

"Who is Creepy Carl? I don't even know who that is."

"Yeah, you do," Victoria said, drawing Amelia's attention. "He's the guy who slammed into you your first day here. When I talked to you."

"The guy who looks like he should have graduated at least three years ago?"

"He should have graduated, but he keeps failing. He doesn't care about grades because he makes bank selling to kids," Darius said, his mouth turning down in a frown.

"Selling? What—" Amelia stopped. "Oh."

"I heard after this year, if he doesn't pass enough to graduate, they're going to make him leave," Jakkie said. "He's been here longer than any of us, than any other student. Would have been nice to go here without him creeping us out."

"If he's dealing, why do they let him stay? If everyone thinks he killed our neighbor, why isn't he arrested? If—"

"Because it's easier – safer – to let him do what he wants," Drake said, hating every word of it.

Amelia stared, wide-eyed and not blinking. Then she closed her eyes and a shudder moved through her body. She dropped her head forward onto her bag, silent.

Chapter Eight

"MAN, SCHOOL IS GETTING SO POINTLESS. JUST GIVE US THE STUPID diploma already." Joaquin bounced the basketball off the cracked concrete to Andrew.

None of them ever actually said it out loud, but Mondays were Guy Night. The only thing that changed was the location. This week was Drake's and they were catching a few hoops before ordering pizza.

"Forget school. I can't stop thinking about the target Amelia brought around." Andrew bounced the ball at Drake. "Creepy Carl already has it out for me."

Drake gripped the ball between his hands and studied it before bouncing it off the concrete a few times. "It's not like she meant to do it. You saw how she reacted to the whole thing." Drake passed it back to Joaquin.

"Why would you think Amelia is on the defensive?" Andrew asked.

"Well, she's the new girl." Joaquin started dribbling the ball.

"Who ticked off Creepy Carl on her first day here." Andrew balled his fist, but Joaquin threw the ball at him, forcing him to either catch it and relax or get hit in the chest.

"You heard what she said. To them it was right. It's what you're supposed to do."

"Well, to us it could mean doomsday!" Andrew said louder, bouncing the ball hard so it nearly hit Drake in the face before he caught it. Drake was driven to defend Amelia, no matter what Andrew said. If he didn't no one would.

"You're not worried about Amelia. You're worried about you."

"Damn right." Andrew stopped and stared down at the ball between them. "But I'm worried about her, too."

"She didn't know who killed the woman next door to her. She just knew they were dead. Or at the least, hurt really bad." Drake paused. It was all in the wording. Say one thing wrong and Andrew would go off again. "Do you really think Amelia would do this on purpose? She doesn't know Carl has it out for you, or why."

Andrew nodded. He uncurled his fingers. "We need to keep it that way. The less she knows, the better and safer everyone will be."

Drake nodded.

Joaquin bent and picked up the ball, tucking it under his arm.

"Dude, Drake, you like her."

Drake never thought Joaquin, of all people, would figure it out. He wasn't about to deny it, but he wasn't going to confirm it either. He was safer that way. Plausible deniability.

"Well?" Andrew questioned. He crossed his arms over his chest waiting for an answer.

He was stuck

"I plead the fifth." Drake knew that gave him away, and even if he thought otherwise, the look on Andrew's and Joaquin's face told him they got it.

"Dude! I so knew it!" Joaquin bounced the ball to Drake.

Drake caught it. "Am I that obvious?"

"Man, it's all over your face. As clueless as she is, she *is* hot."
Andrew shrugged.

"Hey!" Drake snapped.

Joaquin laughed. "That answers the question. Loud and clear."

"Do you like the new school?" came Jolene's voice through the
phone speaker.

"The school, no," Amelia admitted. "It's just so different."

"It sucks you couldn't graduate here. I don't understand why
your father didn't just get a job around here."

Amelia pressed her lips together to keep herself from respond-
ing. They'd had similar conversations before, her and Jolene. Her
friend seemed to think you could just announce to the universe
what job you wanted to do and where, and it just happened. Stuff
'just happened,' but nothing she asked for.

"I've made friends, so that helps."

"Yeah? What are they like?"

She spent the next ten or fifteen minutes telling Jolene about
the friends she'd made and a little about her classes. She didn't say
anything about the shooting or Creepy Carl or their tiny apartment.
It wasn't worth the grumbling. The conversation felt forced already.
Jolene had been her friend since ninth grade, but when Amelia's
mom got really sick something changed between them. It was like
Jolene was uncomfortable with the fact Amelia's mom was dying. If
anyone had the right to be uncomfortable, it was Amelia.

This was only the second time they'd talked since Amelia and
Da left. Deep down, Amelia thought it might very well be the last. It
probably should have bothered her more than it did, but when
Jolene said she couldn't come to Mom's service because it was too
sad, Amelia had known the end was coming.

So be it.

Jolene promised to talk soon and hung up.

And that was it.

Amelia opened another box and pulled out the contents. This one seemed to be filled with books. Her hair fell over her eyes, and with a huff, Amelia pulled her hair back with an elastic band she had around her wrist. Some of the books were dusty. She assumed they were some of her dads when he was back in college. He kept everything. Amelia had used some of the books, but she never saw the complete collection of Shakespeare's work. She went to the couch, sat, and set the book on her lap. She figured she'd take a break and read her mom's favorite scene from *A Midsummer Night's Dream*. She found the play in the table of contents and opened to act one. There was a photo of her mother and father wedged between the pages.

She picked up the photo with care. It was so fragile, and the last thing she wanted to do was damage it. The photo was when her parents were dating in college. Her dad's arm was around her mom's shoulder and they both smiled wide, almost comically. Her mom held her dad's hand, the one on her shoulder, and a bright new engagement ring was on her finger.

Amelia brushed another wisp of hair out of her face and stared at the photo. It seemed so long ago her mother died, and yet it felt like yesterday. It practically was. They'd buried her just a few weeks before, then packed up their former life and moved on. No, not moved on. Just...moved.

Amelia told herself she needed to be able to keep going with her life. It was something her mother would have wanted her to do. She loved her mother with all her heart and she missed her just as much, but she knew her mother wouldn't want her to grieve her death so much she couldn't live. Amelia pushed the dusty book off her lap and onto the couch and stood up. She'd found a photo frame earlier with nothing in it. The photo looked like it might fit. It was just finding it in this mess of a two-room apartment.

She had a plan. She was going to frame it and put it somewhere she and her father could see it all the time. Her mother would like that. Still being part of the family while being so far away. Yes, it still pained Amelia to think of her mother as gone, and as much as her logical side said it was a fact of life, it just plain hurt. Her family never really went to church but she liked to think of herself as a person of faith. She imagined her mother sitting under a big oak tree reading *A Midsummer Night's Dream* up in Heaven. That gave her peace.

Chapter Nine

Darius slammed the door behind him and locked it. They were after him. He just had to get through the next door and he would be fine. The chances of that happening were slim, but he had to give it a try.

He ran down the hall checking to see if all the other doors were shut. He never stopped running. He had to make it. The door was heavy. It took all his strength to pull it open. He could do that. Closing it was more of a challenge, and he tried. The first door was broken down. Darius pulled harder on the door. Footsteps roared as they came closer. The door was moving, just not fast enough.

"Hey, idiot!" a voice called. The door was almost closed.

Just a little more.

The door latched and the people were locked out. Darius put his back against the door and slid down so he was sitting. He put his hands on top of his head.

"That was way too close," he said out loud. He was in a room with metal walls. The whole room was bulletproof. One of the perks — the few perks, as far as he was concerned — when your dad used to be a drug dealer. Not anymore, through. His dad now worked *with* the cops.

Which made him a target.

His friends were worried about Amelia MacDonald making an enemy of Creepy Carl and his friends. They had no idea how scary Carl could be. Or what he was really involved in. Or who he considered enemies.

Like the kid of a narc.

Amelia rolled over and the book fell on the floor. Waking up at the loud thump, she jerked and rubbed her eyes.

"You fell asleep," her dad said. Amelia looked up. He was standing above her, smiling. Just like him. Fall off the couch and land face first in the floor holding a massive book, and he smiles.

"Sorry, Da. I was trying to unpack but I found a book," she said. She sat up and picked the book up off the floor by its spine. "Shakespeare," she said, smiling. Her dad nodded.

"That was a good one. Did I never show it to you?" he asked.

Amelia shook her head.

"There was a photo of Mom in it. I framed it. Seemed like the best thing to do."

She stood up and walked over to the newly framed photo and showed it to her Da. She looked at the frame and smiled. Taking it from her, he looked at Amelia.

"Framing it was the right idea."

Amelia didn't see Drake at his locker, so he had to be in the music room. She'd known him long enough to know that was his routine. She got her supplies for the day and went to the music room.

She promised herself this time she wasn't going to make a big scene. She was just going to slip in and listen to the music. Amelia always thought she didn't like the classical stuff her mom played, but she'd figured out she just liked to hear it played live. It was different to watch someone pull the notes from an instrument, and Drake was excellent at it.

She eased open the door and peeked inside. No one was there but Drake, just as always. Once she was inside, she could hear the music with clarity. When she tried to hear it through walls and doors it distorted, but it still managed to be amazing. But once that door opened it was a whole new song. Amelia loved it. She set her bag on the floor and walked down the ramp to the chairs and stands.

Drake played his heart out, giving nothing but his best as always. It was a slow melodic song, not sad but loving. Amelia had never heard it before. She sat in a chair behind Drake. She didn't want to surprise him by just coming around and sitting in front of the master performing. Could be a little bit distracting. Or that was what she was going to say if he asked her about it.

She suspected he'd shown off the first time she heard him play. He hadn't played anything like that since, and that was fine with her. She'd listen to anything. The way he played was so hypnotizing. It drew her in like it was calling her name. She was never one to analyze music, what it means, how it means it, and why the little dots make it mean what it means. It was all too confusing. Another language to her. She didn't have to "speak the language" to know it was beautiful, kind of like listening to someone speak Ukrainian or Italian. She didn't know what they were saying but loved to hear them say it.

She thought a lot about Drake and his music; well, more Drake than his music but his music was right up there.

Drake stopped playing. He let the note sit in him as he always did after he finished a song.

He turned around and looked at her, his violin still resting on his shoulder. "You're not the best at sneaking in," he said with a slight grin.

Amelia shrugged. "I never claimed to be a ninja. Maybe a pirate, but not a ninja."

Drake hung his arms down at his sides, careful not to let the bow or the violin touch the ground. "You have the attitude of a pirate."

"What are you saying?" Amelia demanded, knowing full well he was teasing. She loved to see his panicked face when she acted mad and he wasn't sure if she meant it or not. "You think I'm bad to be around?"

"No, I'm saying you stand up for what you believe."

Amelia nodded. "You best believe it."

"No matter how wrong it may be," Drake added.

Amelia opened her mouth in shock, and snapped it shut just as quickly. "You jerk," she said and punched his arm. Drake shied away but smiled wide, and she knew they were both just kidding.

Even then, she watched the bow in his hand making sure it was safe. By what she'd gathered, the fine arts and music programs in this district were pathetic if they existed at all. There were fine arts schools throughout New York City, and she had no idea what was involved in going to one, but they didn't seem like an easy option. Or maybe it was. She'd come to realize how little she really did know about...well, everything.

She'd never seen anyone in this band room but Drake, and never saw any other kids carrying instruments. Although, there was that one kid with long, straight blond hair that was always in his face who carried drumsticks with him everywhere. She'd heard him play a mean beat on the lockers once day, but other than Drake, he was the only "musician" she'd seen.

"So, how did you end up playing the violin?"

"Do you mean how'd I learn to play in a district where music isn't actually an option?"

Amelia shrugged. "Yeah, I guess I do mean that."

Drake crouched beside the open violin case and laid the violin inside, carefully setting the bow in its proper space. "I didn't always live here."

Amelia tilted her head and sat on the edge of the stepped levels so she was just above him, almost on eye level."

"Like me..."

He wiped the violin with a yellow rag, removing any smudges, but didn't make eye contact with her. "My dad was a commodities trader. When the stock market crashed a few years ago, we lost it all. I don't remember much of the specifics. I was in middle school. At the time, all I really understood was we lived in Manhattan and then we lived here. And it seemed to happen fast. To me anyway. My father hid it for a long time, even from my mother, right up until we lost the house and had to leave. The only thing I could really keep of value to me was my violin."

"Wow. I'm sorry. Da and I moved pretty quick, too, but we didn't own the house we were in. The university he taught at provided it. Everything that was ours we brought with us and it fits in a one bedroom apartment. Well, *fits* might be an exaggeration, but it's all in there." He was done wiping down the violin and set it inside the gold velvet lined case. "Don't they make violins in different sizes?" Amelia asked. She couldn't picture a little kid trying to play a violin the size of his.

"They do, but this was my grandfather's violin, and it was always too big for me until a few years ago." Drake shrugged. "I had a hard time at first, but I learned."

"So you've always played?" Amelia asked.

"As soon as my parents let me pick it up."

He closed the lid, the latches clamping shut with a dual click. She stood when he stood, and when he walked down the risers to his backpack, Amelia was right behind him. She loved hearing him talk, probably more than she loved hearing him play. She asked stupid questions just to hear his reply, and always wanted to slap herself silly when she realized she was doing it. It certainly wasn't something she'd ever done before.

She liked him. She knew that. She had liked boys before, but just not as strongly as this. This was different. He was on her mind ninety percent of the time. Amelia had to fight the urge to stand close to him all the time, to the point where it would seem weird. So she forced herself to take a step back.

"Did Victoria tell you what I told her about my mom?" she asked.

"She said your mom died." He turned around to face her. "I'm sorry. My parents aren't parents of the year or anything, but I know it would be hard to lose one of them. I bet you were really close with your mom."

Amelia swallowed to keep her composure and nodded. She really wanted to get to a point she could talk about Mom to other people and not feel like she choked on the sadness in her throat. "I was. I loved our family. I hate that I don't have that family anymore. But I have Da, and Da has me."

Drake nodded, his mouth turned down slightly. They walked side-by-side toward the door and he brushed his hand over his hair and held the violin case in his other hand. His hair was definitely too long for whatever cut it was supposed to be and now was a mess, some of it sticking straight up from his fingers.

"You just made it worse," Amelia laughed and stepped closer to him again. She tousled his hair with both her hands. "Da's hair is like this and Mom was always trying to get it under control." She ruffled it again. "Still messy, but better."

Drake's fingers wrapped around her arm and kept her from stepping back, looking her in the eyes. Amelia let her free hand drop, staring back. His eyes were so green. Like the grass in spring. Her mouth opened a little. She wanted to say something — anything — but nothing came out.

Drake let go of Amelia's arm, his fingers running all the way to her wrist before he broke contact. He was the first one to move, taking a step back. "We don't need to be late to class," he said, clearing his throat.

Amelia nodded. "Yeah, I can just see Da lecturing me on punctuality." Amelia walked back up the risers with Drake behind her, to the front of the room where she dumped her bag and she hoisted it on her shoulder. "Even if it is Advanced Math."

Chapter Ten

"*INSANITY: DOING THE SAME THING OVER AND OVER AGAIN AND
EXPECTING DIFFERENT RESULTS.*"
~ ALBERT EINSTEIN

AMELIA PUT HER HEAD ON THE DESK. THIS WAS SO EASY IT WAS stupid. Yep, another brain cell just died because of this math class. She never took notes and she did the homework during class. Only because she was lucky enough the teacher put the assignment on the board at the start of the period. But she was only ten minutes into the class and she was done with it and going insane at a painfully slow rate. She mentally screamed when she heard her name be called on for the answer. She picked up her head and scanned the graph on the board.

"Three." She put her head back on the table. The teacher huffed and walked to her desk.

"And what makes you so sure? Where are your notes? Your work?" Amelia was waiting for a ruler to be smacked down on the table like in the movies where the nuns were allowed to beat the children for giving them lip. Amelia sat up and looked at the teacher.

"Two reasons. One, it's the answer. You are looking for the square radical, and it's three. Two, everything you put up equals three. No way around it. I don't take notes because this class is always three. Do you have some weird obsession with three?"

She heard herself talking, and this little voice in the back of her head whispered to rein it in and get a grip, but she told the little voice to shut up. Then she slammed it into a little box and taped it shut. She was normally very polite to teachers, especially since Da was one, and knew it was always better to get them to like her. But this teacher had crawled under her skin since the day she walked into class. She was like a bad rash. And Amelia had too much going on in her head to be in a class that didn't distract her enough to silence the thoughts.

"Ms. MacDonald," the teacher said in that tone she knew was supposed to mean "this is your only warning."

Nine times out of ten, that tone from a teacher was enough. This wasn't one of those nine times. This one the one time. Today was not the day, and she was not the one. She already started; she had to get it out. It was burning her mouth and she *needed* to get it all out. All about this class.

"What, do you have three kids? Are you on the third spouse? This one lasting longer than the other two?" She gasped loudly. "Oh no, I said a number other than three! Whatever shall we do?"

"Amelia, go to the principal's office."

"You know what would make this class better, making it a class. You get angry at me for having my head on the desk, but you'd be fine with other people *standing* on their desks. It seems to me like you're playing favorites. Or singling me out. And it's not nice."

"Go. Now," the teacher demanded, pointing at the door.

The little voice was screaming "Shut up, you idiot," but she was no longer listening.

"So you send me to the principal's office when you can't come back with a valid rebuttal? Or you are just too lazy to think of one. I mean all you do is find equations that equal three. Can't wait for the final exam, I think I'll ace it. But then again you could surprise me and make something equal to negative three. That would change things up."

The teacher stormed back to her desk and Amelia stood up and watched the teacher pick up the phone. "No need to call security, they won't come anyway. I can get myself there. Anywhere is better than here."

She slung her bag on her shoulder as she walked past the other students in the room. They all stared at her. Whether it was because they all wanted to do the same and they never had the guts to, or they thought she was crazy, she didn't know. Actually, she did know. She knew it had to be the latter. No one had guts in this school, which was stupid considering the stuff they all faced just walking there every day. Only the Dragons and Knights had the guts. Amelia turned and faced her teacher when she stopped at the door.

"Next time, actually challenge the class. Four is a good number, too." Amelia walked out. Not what she wanted to say. She wanted to just tell the teacher off once and for all, just to get the last bit of steam out, but logic and reality had kicked in and she knew she was going to have to deal with Da at some point. At least she could be honest and say she held some back.

The signs on the wall pointed the way to the principal's office, and they were the only things on the walls. It really bugged her. The wall was white, freshly painted cinderblock. It was so new and white that the glow almost hurt her eyes if she looked at it too long. They probably had to paint recently because of another love note left behind by *whoever*. She wondered if once upon a time there were posters on the wall about school dances and who was running for senior class president. That was what her old high school was like. She was allowed to think there. She never felt insulted there.

But Drake was here.

And all the other people who had welcomed her here on her first day: Victoria, Jakkie, Joaquin, Darius, and Andrew. That was something. Heck, here it was her everything. She cared about all of them, differently than she cared about her friends at her old school.

Yeah, she cared about them, but even after only being away for a few weeks she didn't feel the loneliness anymore. That was fine. She had been forced to look at things differently when her mother died. She found herself thinking about the people here more and more and fonder than when she was at her old high school. And out of everyone, she thought of Drake the most.

Drake meant more to her than she wanted to admit, even if it was just to herself because admitting it caused more problems than she could deal with right now. She had to think logically, as much as she hated to. He had no time to care for someone more than just friends, and she needed to go to college. She had to get out of this school and she had to do it cheaply; not a lot of money, the less money the better. For Da's sake

Amelia knew money was tight. Her parents were teachers, not bringing in the big money, although her Da held a Doctorate and had been a university teacher. He had been the main source of money, but he lost job when the university shut down. He lost his health insurance almost immediately. He didn't talk about it with Amelia and absolutely not around Mom. She didn't know. They lived in a house, but it was one paid for and provided by the university for their long-tenure teachers. Like Da. And when the university closed, the option to stay in the house was no longer an option. They'd had some time because whoever took on the ownership of the house wasn't about to toss out a new widower and his daughter, but time had been running out. Which is why they'd taken the first apartment they could find. Maybe they could eventually move somewhere better, but for now they had a home because the two of them were there.

Mom and Da had saved money for Amelia to go to school and had started it before she was born. But all she heard was how prices for tuition and meals and everything were going up every year. Another grand here, another grand there. She was not getting anywhere with those scholarship websites. They were great and all, but everyone and their kids was using them, so the chances of her getting a good one was slim. She might swing some tuition help because of her GPA and she'd done well on her SATs, but they only helped. There was a lot left over.

Drake had a talent. He could play his way out of here. He was that good. He seemed more comfortable playing it as a fiddle — he could switch back and forth with ease — but he had to go classical to get a music scholarship. Amelia could see him playing the fiddle, though. On a stage, rocking out, playing some special arrangement from *Pirates of the Caribbean* or *Harry Potter* and just having a blast. But that was later. He had to get out first.

It happened again, another thought about Drake!

He was always on her mind. Everything led back to him. Well, everything good did. Even just sitting at the table at lunch talking to him. Everyone in the group talked to her, but no one had the same effect on her as Drake. Amelia slowed down so it would take longer to get to the principal's office. She needed to think some more, even if it led back to Drake.

Halloween was Friday. Amelia wanted to do something crazy. But only if Drake and the others would go for it. She stopped walking at the principal's office. She knew there was no denying it; she really did flip out in the middle of math class, and now she'd have to face her father. That was worse than the principal any day. She had never really seen her father mad, so it was never on her list of things to see. But she had no idea what would happen at this point. She'd never gotten in trouble at school, and certainly never sent to the principal's office.

She wasn't scared. Well, not scared of the principal or whatever might be behind that door. She was scared of what might happen later. Not to her. She could take that. But she would not put it past this school to fire Da for her actions.

She should have thought of that consequence sooner!

Amelia started to panic. She'd planted the seed in her own head. What if what she just did was a strike against her father? If Da lost this job they would lose the apartment. That would tear her up. Amelia forced her breathing down and she attempted to calm herself. She wouldn't know until she opened the door and went in.

Half of her wanted to turn and run. Pretend it never happened, just go back to class and say they let her off the hook, she was right, and she escaped all penalties. But that would be wrong, and inevitably she'd get caught. As much as it would make her feel good, to get the final jab in before she left, she wouldn't feel better until she actually had to pay for her actions.

The other half of her just wanted to stand there. Not go in. At least she was doing as she was told; she went to the principal's office. She was not in trouble. Her dad was not in danger of losing his job.

She knew she had to go in. She had to keep her head high and try to talk her way out of this mess. That was going to be a lot harder than talking her way into it.

She exhaled.

It had to be done. And the longer she stood there the more she slipped into the amazing hole she dug for herself.

"Mom, please let this be my overactive imagination and nothing will really happen. I know you can't do anything to influence it one way or another, but can you put in a good word for me with God? Especially if I am going crazy and ripping myself apart for no reason."

Chapter Eleven

FOR ONCE SHE WAS EXACTLY WHERE SHE HAD TO BE, AND FOR ONCE she was not talking in circles with a crazy secretary who had no idea what was going on. She sat across the desk from the principal. For once she wished she had had to wait around and explain everything three times to a crazy old lady. But no, the one time she wanted things to be "normal" for this school and have the staff not do their job, they actually did it.

The principal tapped his pen on the desk to get her attention. Amelia jumped and looked at him. He put the pen down and folded his hands. He was playing this up. She knew it.

"Amelia MacDonald, do you know why you are here?"

"Headmaster Weaver, I really think there is a misunderstanding. I simply made an observation that since my time here the teacher has only used examples with the answer of three. I feel that in order for the class to understand the concept we need examples that equal numbers *other* than three."

Amelia kept herself very calm. She might get herself out of this yet. He didn't interrupt her. That was always a good sign. She shut her mouth, figuring she was going to make things worse if she kept talking. None of what she said was a lie. It was true, just in the classroom she'd had a fit about it. Here she managed to be much calmer.

"Headmaster, huh?" he said.

Amelia nodded once. He seemed flattered by it. She figured he could keep the compliment, and if it meant she would have to call him headmaster for the rest of the year so be it. If it saved her butt this time, and maybe anything else that might happen in the course of the year, she was fine with it.

"I got a different story from your teacher. She said you called her names."

Amelia was in shock. Driving her nuts with the number three was one thing, but lying and throwing her under the bus was something entirely different!

"Headmaster, sir, I would never do such a thing to a teacher. You should understand I respect teachers and would never stoop to such a low level." She cringed inwardly. She would not purposely do any of that, but she could only hope the principal would not see it as a sugar coated piece of lie cake.

"I should think so, Ms. MacDonald, since your own father is a teacher here."

Amelia nodded. This was not going where she wanted it to go. Bringing Da into this was not a good sign and she started to feel the panic rush back into her chest.

"Sir, I think this is a problem we should deal with between you and me and not have to bring my Da into this."

Principal Weaver nodded and rested his hands on his desk.

"I like your father. I hired him because he has a good head on his shoulders. But we don't allow problems like this in our school. We already have enough problems to deal with as it is. Your locker for example," he said, using his hand to gesture to an invisible locker behind him.

"The locker seemed fine this morning, Headmaster Weaver," Amelia said, more quietly than anything else she said.

What the locker had to do with her mental breakdown in math class, she wasn't sure, but she was tired of jumping to conclusions. If the principal liked Da, then things couldn't turn out so bad, right?

"I've seen your school transcripts, Ms. MacDonald, so convincing me you aren't intelligent enough to understand what I'm speaking of will not work."

"Sir, pardon my asking, but what does that have to do with my math class?"

"I am advising you to be careful. I would have hoped you would have understood that."

"Oh, I do Headmaster Weaver," Amelia said as she reached down by her feet to get her bag and try to get out of there. It seemed to be going well, except for the mention of Da, but ended fairly quickly.

"I'll make sure of it because I'll be calling your father out of class so we can talk about this now. I'm sure you understand. Clear the air."

Amelia let go of her bag. She wanted to say out loud what she was thinking but decided it was best left in her head, or else she may really be dead soon.

He struggled to first get, then hold, the class's attention. They just didn't seem to want to learn. He was teaching what he was supposed to according to the school, despite his opinion otherwise, but they were not interested. He wanted to introduce something thought-provoking in hopes it would get them...well, thinking. He hated to see youth wasted like this. Seniors reading "To Kill a Mockingbird" was nearly, well, mocking. He couldn't get over it. He hadn't taught below university level in fifteen years, but he knew what students should have been taught before they left public education.

He sat at his desk; the voices of his students grew louder as the seconds ticked by. They were supposed to be working on a chapter summary, but if they could talk for a little bit as a class, he could think of worse ways to get involved.

The phone on his desk rang. *Oh, look, a distraction.* Something new to think about not related to killing a mockingbird.

"Professor MacDonald," he said.

"Good morning Liam. I have your daughter in the office. There seems to be a misunderstanding and I would like to have you down here as we discuss it."

"Yes, Principal Weaver." He sat up straight. Not good. Not good at all. "I will be there once someone comes to watch the class."

He didn't even wait for a response.

What he wanted to know was why Amelia was in the headmaster's office. A study hall aide came in to watch the class and he left for the office. He ran through every scenario he could think of which would have put Amelia in the headmaster's office. Was this related to the threat on the lockers? Was she in danger? Had something happened he didn't know about? The thought quickened his steps.

The headmaster said there was a misunderstanding. What does *that* mean? She got along with all her new friends. She hated her classes, well, was bored really, but the teachers never said anything to him about Amelia being a disruption. Quite the contrary.

Maybe he was overthinking things. That was his job before. He had to overthink things so his students in college would *start* to think. Now that he was teaching high school, that was no longer the case. He wished it was, but no.

Could she be the one causing the trouble? But Amelia was never a child to go out and make trouble. She was curious, like him, and probably too quick to speak...also like him...but her heart was good and she never intended to misbehave. Sure, things tended to fall out of her mouth but never worth sending her to administration, let alone the headmaster.

By the time he reached administration, he was fairly sure he'd thought of every possible scenario, and knowing his daughter he thought he had it figured out. Well, as much as he could. He walked in with a smile for the secretary, but she just pointed him to a door. He nodded and kept walking. Amelia sat at the desk with her chin down and her hands clenched in her lap. He cleared his throat before coming into the doorframe. Amelia raised her head and looked at him. She had a wide-eyed look, not looking in one place for too long. Oh, she was worried.

Not good.

"Hello, Professor MacDonald. Please sit down so we can get to the point and be on our way to figuring this out."

"Certainly." He sat in the chair next to Amelia and smiled. She hadn't looked away from him since he came through the door. She smiled at him over her shoulder, but it was weak and never reached her eyes. Oh yeah, something was up.

"What can I do for you?" he asked.

"Amelia expressed her opinion in math class today, and while your daughter thought the comments to be...helpful...the teacher's impression is different."

"I see..." Liam said, glancing away from Weaver to his daughter. She sort of smiled, raising one eyebrow.

"She isn't in trouble...this time. I'm just letting you know if this happens again, actions may need to be taken."

Liam nodded. Something more happened and he knew full well he wasn't getting the whole story, but at least there were no problems. He glanced over at Amelia; this time her smile was genuine...relieved.

"Thank you, Headmaster Weaver," she said, turning back to the man on the other side of the desk. "I will make sure I discuss with my teachers my concerns in a better manner in the future."

Oh yeah, something happened. Amelia stood up.

"I don't want to be late to my next class." She grabbed her bag and put it on her shoulder. He stood as well, ready to mention the next period was actually lunch, but she was already out the door.

"Thank you for taking me into consideration, Headmaster. We are working through things together."

The principal smiled and extended his hand. "It's good to see, Liam. I know things haven't been easy for either of you these last few months. Considering the circumstances, this is a minor bump in the road." They shook and Liam turned to leave. "If you ever need to call on me for any unruly students, please feel free to send them my way."

"I might take you up on the offer, but as of now I'm hoping to catch my daughter before she goes off to class."

Before Weaver could say anything further, he was out of the office and in the hall. Just as he thought she might, she hadn't taken off but stood with her back pressed to the wall. She looked up and sighed. The end of class bell rang. The hall would be mobbed in minutes, but there was enough time to find out what he needed to know.

"Are you going to tell me what *really* happened?" he asked.

Amelia looked at him, color flushing her cheeks. In that moment, she looked so much like her mother it almost hurt.

"All of the answers are three, Da. *All* of them. Always. I couldn't take it anymore." She let her bag slip off her arm and land on the floor with a thunk.

He nodded and moved beside her. "I get it. Did you feel any better after you said it?" he asked, leaning against the wall, looking over his glasses at his daughter.

"Oh Da, I felt so much better. But..." She rolled her hands in front of her, wiggling her fingers like she wanted to catch hold of something. "...It all just kept coming out."

Liam smiled and looked down at his shoes. He chuckled, remembering a time when his sweet, calm Lily spouted off at a student's father for twenty minutes. Once she got started, especially if it was something she cared about, not much could stop her until she was done.

"I know, petal. You're like your mother in that way."

She grinned and nudged him with her shoulder. "I thought spoutin' off at the mouth came from you."

Her father chuckled and kissed her hair.

Chapter Twelve

DARIUS WAS IN SHOCK. AMELIA IN THE PRINCIPAL'S OFFICE. NO frickin' way.

Class was over and he was walking to his locker before lunch and saw her and her father come out of the office and start talking. Things looked serious. He ran to the lunchroom, forgetting he wanted to go to his locker. He had to let the others know Amelia was in trouble. He burst through the door and scanned the room till he found someone from the group.

"Drake!" Darius yelled.

Drake looked up and around the room in order to find the source of his name. Once he spotted Darius, he waved. Darius shoved past people to reach him.

"Drake, man, Amelia is so screwed!" Darius reached him and as he got there he saw Jakkie sitting at the table looking confused.

"What are you yelling about? Amelia's fine."

"No way. She and her dad were just in Weaver's office. I saw 'em come out."

"Why would she be in Weaver's office?" Drake asked.

"Man, I don't know, but I have seen Jakkie stressed out and I am telling you, Amelia was stressed out. I know that look. So *somethin'* happened."

Drake looked at Jakkie. She shrugged.

"Man, I am telling you something went down!"

"I don't know, Darius. Amelia never struck me as the type to end up in Weaver's office. And if she did, I don't think she did anything. Not really. Don't you think you might be overreacting a little bit?" Jakkie said. She opened her lunch bag and pulled out a sandwich. "And if anything happened, I'm sure we'll find out about it."

Darius was going to say something but another voice cut him off.

"Darius, are you trying to figure girls out again?" He turned and saw Victoria next to him. "Because it's something no man should ever try."

"Amelia looked like you around finals, that's how I know something is wrong."

"And how do I look around finals?" Jakkie asked. She put her bag on the table and her hands on her hips.

"You know, stressed, upset, frustrated, like you forgot to brush your hair that morning."

Victoria choked on her mouthful of milk.

"What?" she asked.

Drake slammed his hand on the table. "Anyway, in order to save Darius here I think we need to talk about something different." He looked around the room and pointed to Joaquin coming from the lunch line. "I wonder is Joaquin remembered to show up to third class today."

Darius rolled his eyes. "Y'all need to get your heads in the game. This could be bad."

"What are you so wound up about?" Jakkie asked.

"Why don't we wait until Andrew gets here before we try to

figure it out? All that stuff with Creepy Carl could have nothing to do with this, or it could. Laying out every possible scenario isn't going to actually answer the question."

"Darius, if this was something to do with Creep we would have heard about it by now. Will you just shut up and eat your lunch? When Amelia gets here she can tell us then, if she even wants to tell us!" Victoria yelled.

"Something's wrong with Amelia?" Joaquin chimed in as he walked to the table.

"No, nothing is wrong with Amelia," Drake said but he sure wasn't convincing Darius. The boy had it bad.

"Don't even, man. Amelia was in Weaver's office with her dad. She looked like Jakkie around finals," Darius explained.

Victoria moaned and rolled her eyes.

"We aren't even around finals. Don't insult Jakkie that way," Andrew snapped.

"Oh my gosh, will everyone please stop comparing my worrying about my grade point average to Amelia pissing off Creepy Carl?" Jakkie yelled.

Andrew chuckled. "So what is this about Amelia?"

"Last time I'm gonna say this," Darius said, leaning on his hands over the table. "Amelia and her dad were in Weaver's office. I was walking to my locker when I saw them come out and Amelia looked bad."

"Darius, will you just shut up already? We don't know anything," Victoria snapped. "And even if we did, let's not jump to conclusions. We have enough problems without making up more."

"Has anyone heard any rumors going on about her? We might be able to find out something if we ask around," Andrew said.

Darius nodded in agreement.

"Will you knock it off?" Victoria said to Andrew. "God, I swear you boys think you're so manly and can take on the world. Well, guess what? If it Creep, and he'd done something, we would have heard about it by now. And we haven't, not even through the grapevine. Nothing happened worth getting your boxers in a bunch."

"Darius and Andrew have a right to be worried. I mean there's always the threat left on the lockers," Joaquin said. "We all should keep an eye on her."

Darius nodded again. He loved it when his friends agreed with him. It seemed like he really wasn't crazy.

"We are not going to win with any of you, are we?" Jakkie said. She rested her elbows on the table and weaved her fingers in her hair. "If you guys didn't make such a big deal out of everything we might have a normal life."

"Jakkie, if you knew only one of us, you would still never have a normal life. We are all freaks," Drake said.

"Well, you, Amelia and I are the lesser of the freaks. We don't over think every single thing."

"Overthinking could be a good thing. At least it means we're thinking," Drake said.

Jakkie nodded her head in her hands. "Yeah, but everyone is crazy. And I don't want to deal with Creepy Carl."

"I know, and I agree with you. We have to talk to Amelia before we start arming ourselves," Drake said.

"I don't know about you but I think we need to start thinking of a plan." Darius pounded his fist into his hand.

"Plan for what?"

Darius turned around and faced Amelia, who had just walked up to the table. "To save you. I mean, if you were in the principal's office it had to be bad—"

"And Creep related," Joaquin finished for Darius.

Amelia looked at them, clearly confused. "I was with Weaver but nothing Carl related."

"Then why were you there?" asked Andrew.

"I freaked out in math class. Teacher broke the camel's back." She shrugged.

"What?" Darius asked.

"The final straw," Drake explained, looking at Amelia, not Darius.

Darius opened his mouth, then clamped his jaw shut and nodded. He got it now. Darius may not be the sharpest knife in the drawer, he knew that much, but he usually caught on.

"You have the one who uses three, right?" Victoria asked. Amelia nodded. "Oh, then I completely get it. She drives me nuts."

"Wait, wait, wait, you were sent to the principal's office because you freaked out over the number three in math class?" Darius asked.

Amelia paused, then nodded. "Yeah, that's about it."

"Then why was your dad there?"

"How do you know all this?"

"I was in the hall and saw you and him come out of the office. I figured somethin' wasn't right, 'specially the way you looked."

"So you spread around the group that I was dragged into the office with Da over Carl?" she asked.

She opened her school bag and pulled out a plastic bag. Darius assumed it was her lunch. She walked around the table and sat down next to Drake. Joaquin and Andrew nudged each other and Drake looked ready to punch the both of them. Darius figured he was missing something again. He would ask later when his life wasn't being threatened by a girl whose dad worked at the school.

"Not that you *are*, but something happened. I mean after the locker think everyone has been on their toes."

Amelia nodded.

"More like *he* has been on his toes. Yeah, we're all worried about you — worried about Creep — but he's been crazy," Drake said.

Amelia nodded. She seemed to take this all so well. Delinquents writing on the wall, fine. We think she is in trouble, okay. Was she up to something? Darius shook the thought out of his head. He was not one to intentionally cause problems but things happen. He felt bad for thinking it.

Chapter Thirteen

"Weeping may endure for the night, but joy comes in the morning."
~ Psalms 30:5b

Another day, another time to deal with the teacher's homework and anything else that may come her way. Amelia walked through the hallway on the way to her locker before school started. Amelia got to her locker and opened it. She never was good at turn locks, and she never left anything important in her locker, so by not locking it she didn't have to bother with combinations. Just books for class. Those went missing enough in any school, but in this school, she doubted anyone would even care.

A paper fluttered out of her locker when she opened the door. She waited to get it until it fell on the floor since she wasn't about to call attention to herself trying to catch it. It landed face up. Amelia kicked her bag into her locker and read the paper. It was an advertisement for a petting zoo coming into the city. It was going to be in town in mid-November. In fact, the next Saturday.

"Well, that would be fun" she spoke out loud.

Victoria came up next to her. "What would be?" she asked

"There's a petting zoo coming into town this weekend. I think it would be fun if we all went." Amelia handed Victoria the flyer so she could set her bag up for her classes before lunch.

"Where'd you find this?" Victoria asked.

"It fell out of my locker. I figured since I don't have a lock on this thing some one thought it was empty and shoved it through the top slots." She stood up and looked at Victoria. Victoria was still looking at the flyer. "Why?"

"Just wondering." She handed the paper back to Amelia. "I have to do some shopping with Mom and she makes it a weekend deal with all her couponing crap. I would like to, but Mom is crazy about spending time together."

Amelia nodded and only let herself dwell on the idea of how much she'd love to go shopping with her mom, coupons or not.

"No worries. I understand. I'll still ask the rest of the group." She put the flyer in her bag. "Hey, don't let me forget at lunch when everyone shows up I have an idea for Friday. You all might think it's stupid, but I think it'll be funny."

"Amelia, stupid and funny is just about all of our middle names. I think it'll go over fine." They both shifted books and papers. "Hey, I have kind of an out there question."

"Okay." Amelia responded. She shut the locker and used it as support when she turned to look at Victoria.

"Do you like Drake?"

Amelia scowled. "Well, yeah, I like Drake."

"No, I mean do you *like* Drake?" Victoria asked.

"What, are we in kindergarten?"

"At least you know what I mean. I've seen you hanging out with him, sitting next to him and just going out of your way to be around him. Thought I'd ask." Victoria shut her locker and leaned against it.

Amelia mulled over in her head what to say. She did, but should she admit it? Maybe if she started to admit things, more would happen. She wasn't saying she was going to go out tonight and marry him, but maybe she could see if it was mutual. At the thought of marrying him, she smiled at the memory of her father's "You could be the next Bridezilla" joke.

Ahh, what the heck.

"Okay, yeah, I kind of do."

"Kind of?"

"Oh goodness, no third degree, please. Yeah, I *really* like the guy, and yes, I am going out of my way to be around him." Amelia scowled. "I just hate I was that obvious."

Victoria smiled, an almost evil grin.

"I didn't break any cardinal rule of the gang, did I?" Amelia joked, hoping to divert some attention off her, but Victoria didn't seem to be buying it.

"Oh, please, no. We've all been waiting for over a year for Jakkie and Darius to own up to their mutual admiration society" Victoria bounced on the balls of her feet and pulled her lower lip through her teeth.

"Go ahead and tell Jakkie," Amelia said, waving Victoria off. "You know you want to, and I don't want to have to deal with these questions Again." Amelia smiled. She picked up her bag from the floor and put it on her shoulder. "Since we brought up Drake, I'm going to excuse myself and go watch him play his violin." She turned and walked away.

"Oh, don't worry, I'll let Jakkie know," Victoria yelled.

Amelia smiled. She knew Jakkie would know in the next ten seconds. Victoria was like that. She picked up her bag and slung it over her shoulder, turned, and froze. At the end of the hallway, staring at her from under the brim of his hat, his face cast in shadows, was Creepy Carl. He leaned against the wall, just staring. Then one corner of his flat lips curled up in a smirk and he raised one hand, pointing at her, then mimicked pulling a trigger.

Amelia's heart started pounding and she turned in the other direction. Her locker was a straight shot down the hall from the music room. A quick walk and she was there. And one of the best things was Drake was always there.

She didn't hear any music as she approached, and she hesitated before reaching for the door handle. She glanced behind her to confirm Carl hadn't followed and toed up to look through the little wire enforced glass window to see inside. He was in the room, but not playing. She watched through the window of the door. If he wasn't, playing he'd know she came in. If something was going on he didn't want her to know about then it wasn't her place to bother him.

But Carl was in the other direction. And her head told her something was wrong with Drake. It was just weird to see him not playing in the center of the room. The case was there, and it was open. She could not see if there was anything in it but it was there. Drake sat with his back facing the door and he was hunched over, his head bowed down and his hands folded in his lap. She reached for the handle. She knew she should walk away from the door and let him have his time. But she wanted to be there, with him. The urge to go to him was too overpowering.

The door creaked as it opened. Drake didn't move. She dumped her bag in the normal spot next to the door and walked down a few steps before she said anything.

"Drake?" He shifted in his seat and faced her. His face was red. It didn't look like he had been crying, but there was no doubt in her mind he was upset. "Are you okay?"

It was a stupid question. She hated being asked that one stupid question. She always connected it to her mother's death. She hated the question then, and since then it was all she could think about when those words came out of anyone's mouth. Drake pursed his lips like he was going to say something.

She took a step closer and he looked away.

"I was accepted at New York School of Music," he finally said, his voice rough and way too low to be right.

"That's good, isn't it?"

Drake shrugged and cleared his throat. "They let me know I was on the shortlist for a full scholarship for the violin. Only a few accepted students each year get the scholarship." Drake paused. He sucked his top lip in between his teeth.

Amelia stood rooted in her spot.

"I didn't make the cut. No scholarship. I was accepted to attend, but at full tuition, and we know I can't afford that. I tried to convince them, but they'd made up their minds. So now—." He stood up and kicked the case closed. "I don't even know why I bothered."

When he raised his head and looked at her, the look in his eyes broke her heart. Amelia ran over to him and embraced him in a hug.

"Don't say that, Drake," she demanded against his shoulder. "You are so gifted and just amazing, and it's their loss."

Drake finally wrapped his arms around her and hugged her back, pressing his face into her hair. He inhaled deeply and held onto her so tight she could barely breathe, but she wasn't about to tell him to let go.

"What else can I do?" he asked, not taking his face from her hair. His voice was muffled but his breath was warm against her throat.

"Well, why did you start playing?" she asked. It was odd having a conversation like this, but not unpleasant. She smiled and squeezed just a little tighter.

He didn't answer right away, and she thought she felt his fingers stroke her hair.

"I don't really know. I like the fiddle more than the violin. I always wanted to play like I did for you that first day. But for school, in order to go to college, I had to do classical."

"Then play the fiddle."

"It's different. I have to string it differently and it's complicated," he said. He dropped his arms, ending the hug. Amelia took a step back. "I'd have to buy new strings and probably adjust the bridge. That costs money."

"That school is stupid. They don't know what they're doing." She paused, debating if she was going to say what she wanted to. "And there are other schools. Other universities and fine arts colleges or community colleges. If the university where my dad taught was still around, I'm sure they would have taken you."

Drake shook his head. "I have been trying for over a year to get into a school and only one has looked at me, and now they're turning their backs. There's just no college for me right now."

"Oh, no. I expect you to be the next famous reject," Amelia said and pushed his arm. Drake looked at her, scrunching up his brow like he did when he didn't understand, which wasn't very often. "Don't know how about famous rejects?" she asked.

Drake shook his head. She understood, not many people did, even if they were geniuses.

"I can think of at least a dozen famous people who were rejected again and again before they made it big. Walt Disney. Oprah Winfrey. Steven Spielberg! Stephen King. Even Albert Einstein."

Drake still had that weird wrinkle in his brow. "How do you know all this?"

"I did a paper on it when I was a sophomore." He still stared. Amelia sighed and rolled her eyes. Was he just playing stupid? "Moral of the story, never give up. It might pay off in the end." She shrugged. "I sound like something from Sesame Street, but you get the point."

Drake laughed.

"Yeah, you do a little bit. I'll be honest that I applied at other places, but I didn't realize how much I was pinning my future on this school until they disappointed me. I guess I could buckle down and really dive into applications."

"No offense, but that's stupid. I always wanted to go to the university Da taught at. But I looked at others, in case something happened or I wanted to do something different." She shrugged. "Honestly, right now I don't know what I want or where I want to go."

Drake nodded, and she liked that his face wasn't as red and he looked like he understood what she was trying to say. He smiled at her.

"Thank you, Amelia. I'm glad you're the one who found me."

Amelia smiled as Drake walked toward her and stood just in time for him to wrap her in another hug.

"Hey, I have a random question," she said looking up at Drake who was still hugging her.

"Please tell me it doesn't have anything to do with college or my violin," he pleaded.

"Nope. So are Darius and Jakkie dating?"

"No, but they should be."

"Ahh, so you see the romance too." She pushed herself out of the hug and sat in the chair behind her.

"I may be a guy, but that doesn't make me stupid," Drake said.

"I know you're a smartie, but I needed to make sure I wasn't the only one thinking they should get together. And Victoria pretty much confirmed it for me this morning."

"Then, yes, they like each other but they are too chicken to do anything about it."

Chapter Fourteen

RUMOR(N): TALK OR OPINION WIDELY DISSEMINATED WITH NO DISCERNIBLE FORCE; A STATEMENT OR REPORT CURRENT WITHOUT KNOWN AUTHORITY FOR ITS TRUTH

"I'M TELLING YOU, AMELIA *TOLD* ME SHE LIKES DRAKE," VICTORIA barely managed not to yell. The rest of the group looked at her like she had three heads. "I asked her, we had a whole talk about it. She's fallen for Drake."

Jakkie rolled her eyes. "God, why am I the voice of reason?" She sighed and put her hand on the lunch table. "Victoria, we talked about this the other day when Darius thought Amelia was in a gang or something. We can't jump to conclusions."

"I'm not jumping to any conclusion. I'm telling you I asked her and she said yes." Victoria rolled *her* eyes this time. "God, Jakkie, I'm not incompetent. I asked her flat out. She didn't answer at first, but then I figured she decided we'd figure it out anyway, so she said yes. No conclusion jumping, flat out answer."

"Dude, how trippy is this?" Joaquin asked out loud.

Andrew nodded. Victoria looked over at the two boys.

"What do you mean?"

Joaquin and Andrew looked at each other, smirking. Ugh! Boys! Talking with monosyllabic grunts or stupid grins, leaving the girls out there in the cold trying to figure things out. And they wondered why girls get so stressed out.

"Fine. I'll say it," Andrew said. He uncrossed his arms and looked at Victoria, Jakkie, and Darius. "A couple weeks ago, Joaquin and I had pretty much the same talk with Drake. He likes her, too." Andrew shrugged.

Victoria went wide-eyed. "Oh my God, we could totally set them up!" She bounced on the balls of her feet.

"Victoria—"

"Jakkie..." she countered. "Don't you think they look so adorable together?" Jakkie paused. Victoria licked her lips in anticipation. She knew she was right. If not for the fact they met each other only a few weeks ago, they would already be dating. They were so perfect for each other.

Jakkie sighed. "Fine, I guess you're right. I'm not saying we have to set them up, but they do like each other."

Victoria pumped her fist in the air. "Yes!" She pulled out a chair and sat. "Okay, Amelia showed me this flyer about a petting zoo coming into town. When she asks you to go, say no," Victoria started. "And boys, make sure Drake can go." She sat down and waved her hands as she spoke. "Oh! Or since I really can't go this weekend, Jakkie, you go with Amelia and one of you boys can go with Drake, but in a way they don't figure it out."

"That is a little elaborate," Jakkie said.

"Honey, elaborate is my middle name. Remember, Drake is smart, he will figure out something is up. So if we make it look like nothing is going on, it will totally work." She turned and faced the boys. "Now which one of you is going to sign up to go to a petting zoo with Amelia and Drake this weekend?" None of the boys looked at Victoria. She cleared her thought. Still no eye contact. "Andrew, I know for a fact you are free this weekend, so you can go with them. The rest of you, make something up so you can't go."

Andrew sighed, Joaquin and Darius smiled. Victoria had a funny feeling they didn't want to go. Meh, whatever, as long as someone went and made it look better, she didn't care. She looked around and saw Drake and Amelia walking to them. They were talking about something, and were both smiling. "You better think of it soon because they are on their way over here now." The boys quickly sat down at the table and made a pathetic attempt at looking like they were talking. They didn't do 'act natural' well.

"Hey, guys," Amelia said, waving as she came up to the end of the table.

"Hi, Amelia," they all said at different intervals. Drake did the typical male head nod.

"So I was at my locker today and this paper fell out. It was an advertisement for a petting zoo coming into town this Saturday. I already talked to Victoria about it and she can't go, but is anyone else interested in coming?"

Jakkie spoke first. "Oh yeah, Andrew and I were planning on going out there anyway this weekend. We can tag along," Jakkie said with a smile on her face.

Amelia smiled back. "Great, any one else?"

"I might as well come, save Andrew from the girls' 'ohs' and 'ahs'," Drake said. Joaquin and Darius mumbled some reason why they couldn't go. Something came up with family. Allergic to all animals except dogs. That sort of thing. Victoria smiled. This was working out the way she wanted. Soon they would live happily ever after.

"So, I also got this other idea," Amelia said, then paused. "Halloween is Friday. I say we dress up as mascots from insurance agencies and blast the theme songs as we walk by."

"I don't get it." Victoria shook her head.

"Like someone could tape fake money all over them and be the money you could have saved by switching to that insurance company with the little British lizard."

Drake chuckled, watching Amelia. Victoria grinned. Geez, the guy sure could look sappy. He had it, for sure, and he had it bad.

"Oh gosh, no, I'm not doing that," Jakkie said.

Everyone but Drake mumbled agreement to Jakkie's response.

Amelia made a face and crossed her arms with a huff. "Okay, fine. It was an idea. I thought it was funny."

The zoo was in a vacant lot. There were animals everywhere, barking and neighing and bleating and chirping and all the different kinds of noises a farm could have. Plus it was October and the air was starting to smell like cooler weather. The leaves were changing to yellows and brown. It just made everything perfect. Like the cherry on top of the sundae.

The four of them walked around and would stop to pet the different animals. Amelia pushed them toward the animals they didn't want to go to. Like the llama. Andrew didn't want to go near the llama but Amelia forced him. Goats and donkeys and baby horses. Everyone seemed to have fun.

"Andrew and I are going to go back over to the bunnies," Jakkie said, tipping her head back the way they came. "There's a brown one calling my name."

Amelia nodded, staring at her friend. Jakkie had been acting weird since they met up. Not like something was wrong weird, but like she knew a secret weird.

"Sure. Drake and I'll try to stick around here until you guys come back."

Andrew nodded to Drake, and vice versa. Jakkie grabbed a fistful of Andrew's jacket and pulled him away. As soon as they disappeared into the crowd, Amelia took a step ahead of Drake.

In one long stride, he was beside her. "Where are we going to head now?" Drake laid his hand on her shoulder. Amelia did the best she could not to jump right out of her skin. *Oh my God, he's touching me!*

"I thought I saw a sign saying they had reindeer." Amelia decided to grab hold of her courage and took Drake's hand in hers, lacing their fingers through each other's. She pulled Drake through the crowd in search of the deer. Drake stopped, pulling her back to him.

"Amelia, they're right here." He pointed with the hand intertwined with her own. The hand he hadn't let go of since she sucked up her courage and took it.

"Oh, I walked right past them."

Not that she was distracted, or anything!

They walked to the gate and handed the man one of the tickets. He smiled and opened the gate and they walked into the pen. Baby deer, not even big enough to have antlers, were jumping around and playing with each other, then scampering back to the people inside the pen to nuzzle and beg for nibbles of the pieces of fruit and vegetables available to feed them. Drake let go of Amelia's hand and dropped to his knees to pet one of the baby deer. Amelia smiled watching him pet the little animal, then looked around the pen. One deer lingered on the other side of the pen against the wall, away from the others, lying on the hay-littered ground with his legs curled under him. No one pet him or fed him, and he didn't play with the other deer.

Something tugged at her, and she brushed her way through the prancing deer to where the lonely deer kept himself separate from all the others. She spoke softly, making little cooing sounds as she approached, and lowered to her knees in front of the wide-eyed deer. She stuck out her hand for the deer to smell.

"What are you doing?" Drake asked behind her.

"Petting the deer. He's all alone," she said softly so she didn't frighten him. The deer shoved its head in her hand and she pet it.

"Why this one?"

"Because it's alone," she said again, looking up at him. "He reminds me of Rudolph, minus the red nose."

Drake came beside her and crouched. "How do you figure?"

"Rudolph was alone. He was made fun of and left out. Like this guy." Drake reached out his hand to pet the deer as well. Amelia smiled, watching him. "He's the misfit."

"So he's the weird one?" Drake said.

Amelia nodded. "But weird is such a harsh word. Think of the deer as us."

"How are we like Rudolph the Red Nose Reindeer?"

"Goodness, Drake. It's a metaphor. The deer is left out because he is not like the others. Like us. I'm not saying we're left out, but we don't fit in. I'm fine with that. I personally would rather be who I am and not fit in than change who I am and fit in, but the deer here isn't able to."

"I'm not getting it."

"*Rudolph the Red-Nosed Reindeer and the Island of Misfit Toys.* The elf who wanted to be a dentist. Charlie in a box—"

"You mean Jack in a box—"

"No, I mean Charlie in a box. That's why he was a misfit. And birdfish, a cowboy who rides an ostrich, a train with square wheels. Have you not seen the Claymation classic?"

He shook his head in answer. "Do you know them all?" he asked with a chuckle.

Amelia didn't even pause. "A water gun that squirts grape jelly—"

"Grape jelly?"

"You keep interrupting."

"I'm sorry." He didn't look repentant at all. In fact, he was smirking.

"Did you know there was even a depressed rag doll?"

"I didn't, but I get it now."

The baby deer stood, pushing up on its back legs first and then front. Amelia put her hand under the muzzle of the deer.

"Glad you finally got it." The deer rubbed its head in Amelia's hand and galloped off to where the other deer played.

"I don't think he was a misfit. I think he was just sleepy," Drake said.

Amelia shrugged. "Or maybe he needed someone to notice him before he joined the group. You know, give him support."

Drake's fingers laced through hers again.

Chapter Fifteen

"DA, WHAT ARE WE DOING FOR THE HOLIDAY THIS YEAR?" AMELIA called out. She stood in the kitchen pushing all the pots and pans that still hadn't found a home into the cabinets and out of the way.

"Well, I want to keep it the same to a point," he said, looking up from the dish dried.

Amelia looked at him, confused. "Da, keeping it the same means you're talking over thirty people in a two-room apartment."

"Not like *that*," he said, pulling a face. "It'll be smaller, much smaller, but the same food and everything."

"How much smaller are we talking?"

"Well...us. We might be able to get a few other people in here, but it won't be as extravagant as we're used to having. A much smaller meal." He put the dishes in the cabinet and crossed the small space to Amelia. "I was thinking we could do it on the twenty-eighth. Not Thanksgiving and not Saint Andrew's Day, either."

Amelia nodded.

"Okay, that works."

Amelia loved her father's Scottish roots, loved having so many different influences in her life from both him and her mother. They celebrated Christmas and Chanukkah, Thanksgiving and Saint Andrew's Day, Hogmanay and New Year's Eve. Her parents never turned down a reason to have a party, and combining holidays just made them all that much bigger and better. Saint Andrew was the patron saint of Scotland, and according to legend he was the brother of Saint Peter and became a disciple of Jesus. He died for Scotland on an 'X', not on a cross like Jesus or Peter. It was because he died on the X the Scottish put the X on their flag.

Amelia had heard the story from the time she was a little girl.

And since she'd been a little girl, the holidays had been her, Da, and Mom.

This year was going to be tough. In so many ways. It had only been a few months since they lost Mom. That was the worst of it. Dad losing his job, that sucked, but she knew Da would trade any job in the world to have her mom back.

Having both happen just wasn't fair.

Her dad would never say it out loud, because he probably thought he was protecting her in some way, but she knew he'd taken a huge cut in pay to come here, their new home a testament to that fact.

Amelia was a nosey kid, and when she wanted to know something, she dug until she found it. While digging for information about her mom's teaching she'd found statements for her funeral. Just like he'd always done, her Da had taken care of her mom, even in death. But it had destroyed whatever cushion he'd had left. Maybe leaving just enough to take care of them until this job, or another job, came along.

Sometimes she got mad at it all. Not mad. Furious. If her mom hadn't gotten sick, she wouldn't have died. If she hadn't died, even if the university still closed, their family would be whole. She wouldn't be thinking of holidays without her mom, or what she'd lost. She wouldn't be sitting in a tiny apartment wondering how to celebrate holidays with only two-thirds of her family.

Amelia shook it off. She was happy now. She was with her father and both of them were healthy. She could deal with everything else as long as she at least had him.

Her dad always looked on the bright side of things. Took the chance to learn something and see the silver lining. Just like when he met the music teacher at school, Mr. Love, and he told the teacher he was going to teach him how to *really* dance. Whatever *that* meant. Amelia had bumped into the two of them in the hall. Mr. Love was trying to show Da how to jerk dance and Da was trying to teach Mr. Love how to Scottish Step dance. Amelia watched for a moment as her dad made a fool out of himself, and cursed at herself later for not having the brains to take out her smartphone and record it all. She had been too mesmerized.

Yeah, let's go with mesmerized.

"What're you grinnin' at?" her father asked, taking a package of cookies from the cupboard.

"Nothing," she said with a chuckle and sat at the table while Da retrieved two glasses and the milk.

Amelia dug into her backpack and pulled out a notebook, making a list of things they would need to get at the store before the holidays. If they were doing a combination of both holidays, then she was going to choose her favorite parts of each meal.

> *Roasted lamb shoulder with onion*
> *Cullen Skink soup,*
> *Vanilla Rice Pudding*
> *Winter fruit.*

Her mouth watered and she picked up one of the cookies, but it didn't compare to the Scottish treats. All the food she loved.

Cranberry Sauce
Sausage Stuffing

She paused, tapping the pencil against her cheek. Most of this was traditional Scottish holiday food, but she wanted some of Mom, too. She smiled and kept writing.

Sufganoit — find a recipe or a Jewish deli/bakery
Matza Ball Soup
Challah bread

It all sounded so good, she was half tempted to walk down to the store now and go get the food. But she would have to wait till it got closer to the time. Only another week to go.

"Hey, Da, can I invite some of my friends over for the meal?"

He paused, a cookie halfway in his mouth. "You think they'd like our kind of party?"

Amelia grinned. "It sure would be like nothing they'd ever seen before. They need some culture around here," she teased.

Da shrugged and bit the cookie, talking around the food in his cheek. "Sure, if you think they'd like it."

"I think they would like it."

"And Jolene?"

She shook her head. "I don't need to ask. She wouldn't come."

Da didn't answer immediately, and she knew he watched her, but she wanted to pass off Jolene's absence like it wasn't anything to talk about. Because it wasn't. Not really. Not anymore. And that was fine. She had six amazing new friends.

"Sounds good to me. I can get to know them outside the class-room." He smiled.

"Thank you, Da" She went back to making her list of food, trying not to think too hard about spending the holiday with Drake.

Chapter Sixteen

"Blessed are thou, Lord, our God, King of the Universe, who by His word brings about all things." ~ Jewish prayer

Lunch seemed to be the main time to bring up anything deemed important discussion. If anything ever happened it was talked about at lunch. Everyone in the school had the same lunch. The only thing that varied was who spoke first. Today, it was Amelia.

"So, Da and I are doing something different this year. We normally celebrate Saint Andrew's Day and Thanksgiving separately, but this year, because of moving and everything else, we're going to do them on the same day. Monday the twenty-eighth. We'll have food for both holidays. Da said I can bring people, so you all can come over to my place next Monday and eat."

"Saint Andrew?" Andrew asked. "I'm good but not *that* good."

"No, Saint Andrew is the patron saint of Scotland," Drake replied.

"Man, just let me have my moment! And how do you know that?"

"I read."

"Wait, your dad's really Scottish? He is not putting on the whole act?" Jakkie asked

"He really is Scottish. What kind of question is that?" Jakkie just shrugged and Amelia shook her head. "If anything, he tries to act American while he's teaching. I don't think he does it very well."

"Wait, why would a British person have Thanksgiving?" Darius asked.

"He's not British, he's Scottish," Joaquin corrected.

"Well, Scotland is part of the UK," Amelia explained.

"But we didn't escape the Scottish!" Darius yelled.

"Guys, focus!" Amelia yelled over him. "So, who's coming for the dinner?"

"Oh heck, yes! I am so there," Victoria practically shouted.

"What sort of food?" Darius asked, apparently calm enough now to rip a bite out of his stale roll, talking around the lump.

"Roasted lamb, cullen skink soup, and vanilla rice pudding," Amelia said, ticking each food off on a finger. "Stuffing, cranberry sauce, and Boston cream pie. And probably a lot of Jewish food, too."

"Jewish. Geez, I thought you said you were *Scottish*," Andrew said.

"My mom was Jewish."

"Wait, so you're having Jewish, Scottish, and American food for a Thanksgiving-slash -Saint Andrews Day dinner?" Darius listed.

Amelia nodded. "Yep, that about sums it up."

"Man, I'm in," Joaquin said. "I don't know what half that stuff was you said, but I don't care. Food is food."

Amelia smiled.

"Well, the lamb explains itself. Cullen skink soup is like fish soup, but creamier. Like chowder, I guess. And the vanilla rice pudding is just that, but it has grilled winter fruit and cinnamon on top."

"Count me in," Darius said.

"Me, too," Drake added, smiling at her.

She'd gotten used to the nice flush of warmth she felt whenever

Drake smiled at her or touched her hand. She smiled back and immediately looked away.

"I'm allergic to fish," Jakkie pointed out. "Can I just not eat that?"

Amelia nodded. "Don't worry. There'll be plenty of other food. We're not going to starve you because you can't eat fish."

"No, Jakkie, they don't want you there now. Cullen skunk soup was the whole meal," Andrew said.

Jakkie stuck her tongue out at him. "It's skink, idiot. Not skunk. I'll be there, too. Looks like the whole gang will be at your house."

Amelia smiled.

"Good. People are just what our place needs."

Shopping for the food was the easy part; this part of New York City had entire blocks dedicated to different ethnic foods. Well, other than the prices. Amelia never realized how expensive lamb was before she was the one buying it. But once she was willing to give up the contents of her wallet, it didn't seem like too bad of a bill. It was a good thing she found some coupons.

Unlike any year before, when she just "helped" her mom in the kitchen – which now she realized accounted for little more than peeling some potatoes and dumping ingredients in a bowl her mother had already measured out — she was the only one cooking the meal this time. That was the hard part. Some smoke and a little fire. Nothing overly bad. And she was able to get it under control quickly, and the meat wasn't burnt too badly. She could chip the blackened part off with a fork.

"That smells great, Amelia. What is that? Charcoal?"

"Funny, Da, really funny," she said, shaking her fork at him over her shoulder. He smirked and leaned his shoulder against the kitchen door jamb. "Just remember who had too many papers to grade to help me out here."

Amelia wiped the sheen of sweat from her face. It was cold outside. Snow had started falling last week and there was a definite chill in the air. The rattling radiators along the walls had worked hard to warm the apartment, but not today. With the oven on and all the burners going, it was plenty warm.

"Oh, what are you going to do? Put something in the food? Remember, you have friends coming over for this meal."

Amelia smiled.

"No, I wouldn't do anything to the food. I've been working too hard on it to throw it all away for a laugh. I have been on the wrong side of a food prank once, remember?" Da flinched at the memory. Someone played a trick and put cayenne pepper in her chocolate milk when she was in elementary school, and she'd spent an entire night in the bathroom throwing up. Both Mom and Da had stayed up with her, neither going to bed. "Plus, you sleep in the bedroom. I sleep on the couch. I'm sure I can get you back any time I want."

"Point taken," he responded. "So when is everyone supposed to show up here?"

"Any minute now. Good thing, too. I just finished the food. Just have to set the table," she said. She looked at her father again. "Or, you could do it for me so I can put the finishing touches on the food."

Her dad groaned. "Do I have to?"

He sounded fourteen instead of forty-four. She grinned but kept her back to him so he couldn't see.

"Da, please," Amelia said, trying to sound annoyed. "Did you do this to Mom?"

"Yes, I did," he said, stepping beside her to kiss her hair. "She was just as amused as you are now. I don't know why. I think it is great."

Amelia smiled. "Well, of course, you think it's great. You're the one causing the trouble."

"Trouble? I think trouble is too harsh. How about gentle teasing?" he said as he grabbed a handful of plates from the cupboard.

When she didn't answer, he popped his eyebrows high over his eyes. "No? Um...annoying?"

"Oh, don't worry. You're that, too."

Her dad gasped. "Amelia, you are so much like your mother. Quick with the one-liners."

"I learned from the best."

"Well, thank you," he said.

"I was talking about Mom."

Her dad looked at her in shock. "Ouch, that one hurt."

"Then don't open yourself up for it."

The intercom to the downstairs building door chimed. Amelia walked over to the intercom and pressed the button. "Bill and Ray's plumbing service for all your plumbing needin' needs. How can I help you today?" she asked.

"Amelia, open the door so we can get in. We're all here, and we're *freezing*."

She smiled at Drake's voice, a different kind of warmth stirring in her chest. Amelia liked it. Whatever direction she and Drake were going, she liked it. So did Victoria. Ever since the petting zoo, she'd told Amelia at least once a day, "I told everyone you would be a perfect couple." Amelia didn't think they were at the couple stage. Heading that way? Yes. There yet? No.

"Dang it, Kirk, I'm a doctor not a doorman," she actually managed to say without laughing.

"Amelia, please. It's cold out here."

"Fine, be that way." She pressed a button that released the main entrance door so the group could get in. It would take them a couple of minutes to reach the third-floor apartment. Amelia looked at her dad who was slowly setting the table. "Come on, Da. They're on their way," she urged.

"I can only set the table so fast," he replied, carefully arranging a fork and knife beside a plate. Even from the doorway, she saw his barely suppressed grin.

"Fine, don't have a proper house for the guests who are coming over for Saint Andrew's Day," she said with a wave of her hand.

"Never thought of it as that. Don't worry; the table will be set by the time they get here."

"Good because they're probably at least on the second-floor landing by now."

"Oh, that is *not* fair," he said, circling the table, the clatter of plates and flatware filling the apartment.

"Hurry up."

Her dad scurried around the table trying to beat the approaching teenagers. Amelia laughed. He'd gone from joker to serious in thirty seconds flat.

"Done!" he yelled, tossing his hands in the air in victory a split second before the knock on the apartment door.

Chapter Seventeen

MAY THERE ALWAYS BE WORK FOR YOUR HANDS TO DO.
MAY YOUR PURSE ALWAYS HOLD A COIN OR TWO.
MAY THE SUN ALWAYS SHINE UPON YOUR WINDOWPANE.
MAY A RAINBOW BE CERTAIN TO FOLLOW EACH RAIN.
MAY THE HAND OF A FRIEND ALWAYS BE NEAR TO YOU AND
MAY GOD FILL YOUR HEART WITH GLADNESS TO CHEER YOU.
~SCOTTISH BLESSING

"OH MY GOD, THAT FOOD WAS SO GOOD. I NEVER THOUGHT I'D LIKE lamb," Victoria said as she rubbed her stomach.

"Okay, I have to agree. It was good food, and I'm the picky one," Darius said.

"Picky?" Andrew gasped. "Darius, you'd eat anything as long as it's free."

"Well, I'm glad you all liked it. Please feel free to thank the chef at any time."

"Oh yeah, thank you, Professor MacDonald, for the food," Jakkie said.

"Hey, *I'm* the one who cooked it all. Not him. He can't cook for beans."

"Oh, no, that's not fair. I can cook beans quite well," he said with faked indignation. "Though, I do love them cold from the tin."

"Cold green beans from the can?" Jakkie said in shock.

"Baked beans," Amelia corrected.

Jakkie made an even worse face but tried to hide it immediately. Drake chuckled. She knew Drake understood. Da tried to make cookies one time for his class and gave one to Drake for a sample. He was sick afterwards. Needless to say, Da didn't give his class the cookies.

"I will gladly take the compliment," Da said.

Amelia rolled her eyes. Today seemed to be a day her dad was going to dish it out more than usual. "You would."

"What does *that* mean?" he asked

"Nothing." She widened her eyes in feigned innocence.

"Oh, I know it means something."

"Okay, I'm not getting in the middle of this." Andrew pushed back from the table and stood. "So, Drake, Joaquin, Darius, are you coming?" All the guys nodded. "Okay, so, we will see you at school tomorrow. If you need us, we'll be at Joaquin' house," he said.

Amelia walked them across the room to the door and hugged them all as they left the apartment and went into the hallway. "I'll see if I can snag a feast of leftovers for lunch."

"Sounds like a plan," Drake said, leaning closer to her to speak, his hand wrapping around hers. "But before you give any to the others, meet me in the music room and we can split the food up as we see fit."

"Don't be so greedy," Amelia said and she pushed him out of the apartment with the other three boys.

"I want some of those Jewish donut things—"

"I'll see you tomorrow," she said, cutting him off by shutting the door.

Amelia walked into the room where Victoria and Jakkie were talking to her Da.

"So your name is really Liam?" Victoria asked.

Amelia sat down. She didn't want to know how this topic came up, but because it was such a random topic she didn't really want to miss it. With Victoria talking it had to be funny. Da nodded.

"Yes, it is. I was named after my Granda," he said.

He set his elbows on the table and rested his chin in his hands. He looked over his glasses at the girls at the table. "Amelia's mother always made fun of my name when we first met. Said it was an old man's name. Well, I proved her wrong when I showed her the time of her life."

Victoria gasped.

"I took her roller skating," he clarified.

"I thought you were going to say something totally different," Victoria said.

Both Jakkie and Amelia slapped Victoria's arm.

"He's my teacher!" Jakkie yelled.

"He's my Da!" Amelia yelled. Amelia folded herself in half and put her head on her knees. "Ewwwww!"

Her dad chuckled.

"What? I'm just saying…" Victoria defended.

"Oh, it's quiet alright I think," he said. "I've been bothering Amelia all day, and I'm just seeing how much I can truly bug her."

"I like your accent," Victoria said, changing the topic. "I've never met anyone from Scotland. You're really from Scotland?"

"With a name like MacDonald I would hope so," he said.

"Oh, that's so interesting. How long have you been in America? You're legal, right?" Victoria asked.

"Victoria!" Jakkie yelled. She put her head on the table. "I *cannot* believe you just asked that!"

"It's fine, Jakkie, I was bound to be asked sooner or later," Da said. "Yes, Victoria, I am legal. I am a Naturalized American Citizen."

"Oh, okay," Victoria said, actually looking relieved.

Amelia looked at the clock on the wall. It was ten thirty. They had been eating and talking since six. Well, more talking than eating. She was glad she made a lot of food because people had gone back for thirds and fourths.

"Do you have any other questions for me?" Da asked, pushing his glasses up his nose. He leaned back in his chair and brought his left ankle up to rest on his right knee, his hands linked over his stomach.

"Nope, I think I got all my answers. Thank you," Victoria said.

Jakkie slapped her palm against her forehead. "Victoria, why do I hang out with you?"

"Because I'm amazing like that." She blinked her eyes rapidly.

"Don't flatter yourself," Jakkie said.

"Okay, that one hurt."

"Good."

The two kept bickering. Amelia watched, ready to break up yet another fight. She was hoping to stop this one before fists were involved.

"Well, I think I'm going to go to bed," Da said with a big yawn. He stretched out his lanky arms for emphasis. "I'll see you two tomorrow at school. Victoria. Jakkie."

To some he was subtle. To Amelia, not so much. But it was to the point enough to get the girls to their feet.

"Okay, bye, Professor MacDonald," Jakkie said. She stood up and pushed Victoria to the door. "Come on, Victoria. Let's head back home and study for school tomorrow."

"But Jakkie, I never study and you know that."

Jakkie slapped her hand over Victoria's mouth before she could say anything else.

"See you tomorrow, Amelia. You better bring leftover food."

Amelia nodded. "I'd be dead if I didn't."

Jakkie nodded and pushed Victoria into the hallway. Amelia shut the door behind them. She walked over to the couch and fell onto it looking up at the ceiling.

"I think I'm slipping into a food coma." She rolled over onto her side and curled up into a ball. "I'm going to fall asleep right here."

Da came to her and put his hand on her head. "I can feel your pulse through your hair. You do need some sleep."

Amelia nodded and batted away her father's hand. "I go sleep now," she mumbled.

"In your school clothing?"

Amelia nodded. Sorta. "Too lazy to move. Don't really care," she mumbled.

"Well, alright then. See you in the morning, Amelia."

"Night."

He dad turned out the light. "You did wonderful, sweetheart. Your mother would be proud."

It was still snowing.

Weeks passed since the Saint Andrew's Day/Thanksgiving meal, and it was still snowing. The plows could barely keep up. They said it was the worst winter they'd had in years. But they still had school. If they canceled one more day because of snow, they'd have to declare a state of emergency and that was not in the school budget. So they went to school.

Amelia walked into the building and shook the snow out of her brown hair. Winter break started the next day after school, so all the work in classes was busy work. Something Amelia was fine with doing. All the work in the school was too easy anyway. Though she had learned to keep her mouth shut during class, so she wouldn't have another fit.

She didn't even walk to her locker; she went straight to the music room. The music had changed over time, slowly so not to attract a lot of people. Drake had switched from violin to fiddle and had worked on more "slap your knee and stomp your feet" pieces. She'd even gotten him to try some Celtic foot stompers and had turned him onto Scrum, her absolute favorite Scottish band. He found a cheap way to string the violin to be a fiddle and had worked a few hours at the music store to earn a new bow. Even Jakkie and Victoria could tell Drake was much happier.

She never kept quiet when she walked into the music room. She would go in clapping her hands and singing the words to the song if she knew them. Today she didn't know the words, but it was a dance-worthy song. She twirled abound and spun herself in the chair in front of Drake. He smiled and kept playing, his dark hair falling across his forehead as he jerked side to side with the beat he created. Amelia shifted the chairs so she could lay down. All the spinning made her dizzy.

Drake stopped short in his song. "What are you doing?"

"Sleeping," Amelia replied as she put her arm over her eyes.

"Why?"

"Because I'm sleepy. And my bag is heavy; it takes too much energy to move." Drake put the fiddle away, clicked the case closed, and picked up Amelia's bag.

"Dang, do you ever clean this out?"

Amelia groaned in response.

Drake opened the bag and pulled out the papers. He came to where she'd stretched out and sat by her feet.

"Why do you still have the flyer from the petting zoo in here?" he asked. He put the paper on the floor next to him with a stack of used-up notebooks, returned tests and homework, and several notices she never bothered to give Da since he'd seen them already by the time she got home.

Amelia sat up, groaning. "Because cleaning it out is too much effort." She leaned against him and rested her cheek against his shoulder.

"Oh, you poor thing," he said in a teasing voice, turning his cheek against her forehead.

"That's right. Pity me."

He chuckled, but stopped short, reaching for the stack of papers he'd just taken from the bag. "What's on the back of the paper?"

Amelia leaned away from him. "I don't know. An old grocery list?"

Drake held it out to her, but read it aloud. "Tick Tock Click Boom. Keep your mouth shut." Drake paused. "Amelia, this has been in your bags for *weeks*."

Amelia looked at Drake. "What the crap does that mean?"

"It means Creepy Carl is still watching you," Drake said, his teasing features from a moment ago completely gone, replaced with angry tension.

She felt the color drain from her fake. Drake leaned toward her. "What? What did you just think of?"

"The day I found the flyer," she said. "I found it and shoved it in my bag. But when I shut my locker, Creepy Carl was at the end of the hall. Watching me. It made me feel cold." She blinked at focused on Drake. "And he..."

"He what, Amelia?"

She raised her hand and mimicked the trigger motion Carl had done.

"Why didn't you tell anyone? Why didn't you tell me?"

"It was the day you were upset about New York School of Music. I was going to tell you, but it didn't seem as important as you."

"Geez," Drake said, raking his fingers through his hair.

"I'm sorry..."

"We have to tell the group. And your dad."

"But, like you said. It's been in there for weeks."

"Exactly," he said, standing. He offered his hand and pulled her to her feet. "Which means he and his buddies have been biding their time."

Forgetting the fiddle, backpacks, and stack of papers in the music room, they ran into the hall looking for their friends.

Chapter Eighteen

\Darius was pinned against the wall, rancid breath in his face. He struggled to get free from Reggie, Carl's muscle, who held him. He hadn't been fast enough this time.

"Awww, is the narc's son scared?" Reggie hissed in his face.

Darius struggled. One thing his dad had always said was if he was ever in this situation, don't say anything. And if you had to, get them distracted. He opted for quiet. They suspected he'd done something, or his father had said too much. Darius didn't even know.

"Hey, ain't he a friend of the kid who called the cops on you?" Matteo, Carl's other ever-present partner in crime, said. The grip holding Darius against the wall tightened.

"You're right, man. So, if we mess with him, we're messing with more than just a narc's kid, but a snitch."

Darius struggled again.

"Just kill the kid and get it over with." That voice he knew.

Creepy Carl.

"I'm bored. Just ice him and we'll go find the girl. I promised her a date."

"Hey, you kill me you're gonna have other problems."

"You talk big for a weak little punk," the voice he didn't know said.

"Tell you what, kid. Run off and tell your girlfriend we're on our way."

Darius hit the floor with a thud.

"We can hit two birds with one stone."

Darius dared not move. At this angle, he could see all the weapons the three of them had on them. "Go, kid. We'll get you later," Carl promised. "Tell anyone we're coming and it won't be just you and the new girl. I'm in the mood to leave this dump with a bang."

He nodded and ran out of the building. He would have gone home and reported to his father, but he had a really bad feeling something was going to go down at school so he ran there.

"Where is Darius?" Amelia screamed, grabbing Victoria's arms. "You have like every class with him. Where is he?"

Victoria shrugged. "We haven't been to any classes yet, so I don't know."

Amelia paused, trying to tamp down the panic that had hit her in the music room. Maybe things weren't so bad. Maybe Carl was just tossing around threats to scare everyone. Maybe they thought it was funny.

Maybe.

Why was this kid allowed to just walk around like he wasn't a damn menace to society?

"Well, what's the worst that could happen right? I mean we don't know anything will happen." Amelia sighed, trying to get all the tension out of her body. She opened her locker and a paper fell out. She was afraid to touch it. Everyone was.

"You had to say something," Andrew said.

Amelia could only stare at Drake, wide-eyed. His face was grim, his jaw clenched when he bent to pick up the paper.

"Today," Drake read out loud.

Amelia covered her face with her hands. This was not good. This was the cherry on the crap sundae.

"Da," she blurted.

She turned and ran down the hall, Drake and the others right behind her. Someone had to know. This was a direct threat and the school had to do something about it. That, and she wanted Da. Call her a child, but something was wrong, and she wanted her father.

Amelia hit the ground with a grunt, Darius holding her down.

"Don't do anything," he demanded.

Amelia pushed him off with the help of Drake, who had ahold of Darius' collar and sat up. "Where on earth have you been?"

"Look, I can't explain right now," he said, shrugging his way out of Drake's hold, "but you can't say *anything* about Creep. You have to trust me. You have to get out of here, but don't say *anything*."

Amelia stared at him. "How did you know?"

"How do I know what?"

"About the threat in my locker. Just like the last one. We're assuming from him. It said whatever is coming it's happening today," Amelia said.

"Wait." Darius paused. "What notes? Last one?"

"Drake found the flyer from the petting zoo in my bag, the one that fell out of my locker weeks ago, and on the back was a threat. Tick Tock Boom. Keep your mouth shut. I assume Creepy Carl put it in there, but I never looked on the back. Today there was another note saying today."

Amelia reached out her hand out for someone to help her up. Drake grabbed hold of it and pulled her to her feet. "You okay?" he asked.

She just nodded, turning her focus again on Darius. "But, you said Carl is coming here today? To do what?"

Darius just winced. "Please. Just leave. If you're not here, maybe it won't be as bad as it could be."

"What are you even talking about, Darius?" Jakkie demanded.

Whether it was perfect timing, or just the universe playing a rotten trick, a gunshot rang out through the school. Amelia jumped and Drake stepped closer to her. Someone screamed, and then the school went silent.

Another shot rang out. Everyone scattered. Drake grabbed Amelia's hand and the group took off running toward the music room. The other students in the halls started screaming and trying to find cover. They reached the music room and Drake pulled on the door.

"Locked! What the hell? We were just here!" he yelled.

The others came to a stop. "Where are we supposed to go now?" Victoria wailed, her hands fisted in Andrew's jacket.

"Well, when they do the drills—" Joaquin started.

Andrew cut him off. "The drills are for lockdowns, stupid. Class hasn't even started yet. They don't cover this." Another gunshot in the background, followed by laughter and shouting echoing through the halls.

"What about Da's room?" Amelia asked.

"Worth a shot," Joaquin said.

"No, it's across the school. We would be in the line of fire," Jakkie said.

They had to yell in order to hear each other over the screaming and the gunshots. They were, in essence, trapped. Amelia's heart pounded so hard it hurt. All she could think about was Da. What if he got hurt? What if she lost him, too? Her eyes burned.

"We can't assume we're the ones they're going for," Amelia said, not even convincing herself.

"Amelia, think about it. They left notes in your locker. And Darius just said—" Andrew said.

"Damn it!" Darius yelled. "Listen to me! Carl and two other guys are coming after you," he shouted at Amelia. "He told me if we don't say anything to anyone, they'd just kill you and me."

Amelia swayed, and Drake put his arm around her, holding her up.

"That's not what it sounds like!" Joaquin shouted back as more shots echoed through the halls.

Jakkie doubled over and covered her ears with her hands.

"He said he was bored." Darius dropped his shoulders, his eyes sad. "You gotta get out of here, Amelia."

"Jesus Christ," Andrew mumbled, tipping his head back with eyes closed.

"Dear God, we're all going to die!" Victoria wailed.

"Not if you leave!" Darius pleaded. "Please, just go!" He shoved Amelia and Drake, then pulled Jakkie to her feet and pushed her to them. "Go!"

There were more shots. A lot of them. Different kinds, like different weapons. Fast. There was a loud bang. It sounded like doors being slammed open and hitting the walls.

Chapter Nineteen

Gunshots rang out around the school. Guns and screaming, and the group were stuck in a wing of the building where one of the only rooms that was ever open was locked. Jakkie took off down the hall, trying every door. One of these rooms had to be open. Amelia watched and pinned herself against the lockers. She willed herself to disappear.

She knew they needed shelter. They had to find a place to hide.

"He told me if we don't say anything to anyone, they'd just kill you and me."

"Da..." she whispered and closed her eyes.

Jakkie came running back. She shook her head no. Stupid teachers. They locked the doors once something went on, but they never thought to consider the students stuck in the hall. Amelia knew her dad would be holding the door open and calling students into his room to make sure they were safe. Here they only cared about themselves. She grew up being taught she should help people, and here she was in the middle of the hallway, knowing someone was going to get hurt and there was nothing she could do to stop it or make sure she and her friends were safe.

She closed her eyes, imagining her father pulling kids to safety, scanning the hallway for her. What if he left his room? What if he went looking for her?

Panic made her heart pound and she had a funny, bitter taste in the back of her throat.

She had no idea what to do. She couldn't talk herself out of this, she couldn't hide. She was stuck and she wished it would just be over already. She wanted to go back in time so she could tell her dad not to call the cops. None of this would have happened if Da didn't call the cops. The bell would go off and she would go to her painfully stupid math class and go on with her life. She would hang out with Drake and the others and nothing would happen. Everyone would go to community college and be friends forever, even after they went their separate ways.

That was Amelia's happy ending. She never dreamed she would be hiding in a hallway from the hatred of one person.

Except, if he hadn't called, he wouldn't be Da.

"So what do we do?" Amelia asked, frustration eating at her. "Do we just stand here and wait for them to show up and blow us away?"

"If you have a better idea then I would love to hear it. If you haven't noticed we're trapped!" Andrew yelled.

"We could at least try to get to Da's room, go a back way. I know he'll let us in," Amelia snapped back.

"No one else will let us in."

She turned at the sound of Drake's voice. It didn't sound like he was hopeful about getting to Da's room, but he also sounded like he knew they were stuck. What do you do in a time like this? Victoria hugged Amelia. She hadn't expected to be hugged, but it was something she needed more than she thought. It was a comfort.

But, she didn't deserve comfort. This was her fault. That stupid call to the police because Creepy Carl killed his girlfriend, or whoever, and now he was Crazy Carl. She set them off. Like a bomb. Once you lit the match it was only a matter of time before the bomb went off. And then, bang, it exploded and caused other bombs to be set off and one by one everyone got hurt. Gunshots, screams and banging kept echoing in the halls. Maybe they were safe where they were. Not many people came down this hallway. Not many people ran down here for shelter. It was a hope.

Then all hope disappeared.

Carl came around the corner, with two guys way too old to be in high school right behind him. They were laughing and smiling, big guns like rifles in their hands. She didn't know what they were, but they terrified her. Drake shoved her in the opposite direction and everyone ran. Everyone except Jakkie. She just stood there like a deer in the headlights.

"Jakkie!" Andrew yelled.

She didn't respond, just stood there looking into the barrel of the gun. If there was ever a time when life seemed to slow down and everything was in slow motion, it was that moment. Seconds felt like a lifetime.

"Yo, loser!" Darius yelled and ran.

"Darius!" Amelia shouted.

"No!" Jakkie cried.

Where was he running to? The hall was a dead end. Maybe it was a hope he could outrun a speeding bullet, but that was only in a comic book. Darius' entire body buckled and hit the floor, skidding forward across the ancient linoleum, in almost the same moment the crack of gunfire went off and threatened to make her eardrums burst. Amelia's knees gave way and she hit the floor, covering her ears with her hands. It couldn't stop the sound because it echoed in her head. She felt sick. Somewhere, really far away, Drake said her name.

Jakkie tried to run to Darius, but Andrew and Joaquin grabbed her. She cried and shoved their hands away to run to him. "Oh my

God, oh my God, oh my God!" she kept saying. Jakkie cried, holding her hands in front of her face with blood staining her fingers. Darius' blue shirt had turned dark with blood. He tried to get up, groaning loudly.

Amelia blinked slowly, trying to find her body again, and stared at Carl. He just stood there with a smile on his face. He walked past Darius, a disgusting smirk on his face, staring at Amelia as he walked. Drake pushed her behind him. Darius tried to move, tried to sit up.

Jakkie put her hand on his arm. "Don't move, Darius. You're hurt bad," she choked out.

Why was Carl just standing there smiling? It seemed sadistic.

"Jakkie, you know I always loved you, right?" Darius said, and the hallway shifted around her while Amelia's head turned by its own will to stare at him. He had rolled onto his side, gripping Jakkie's hand. "I just never had the guts to tell you."

"You just told me, idiot," she said, smiling at him, but it was shaky and tears ran down her cheeks. "Don't talk like you are going to die, because you're not." She shook off her overshirt and pressed it to his back.

"Jakkie..." It was all he said. One word spoke a million.

Jakkie cried harder. No matter how hard Jakkie tried to keep the blood inside his body, it did no good. The wound was high in his back. Darius was having a hard time breathing. And even if they called 911, it would take them too long to get there. There were sirens outside. Someone must have called the cops. For this, they had to come.

"Darius, I love you, too. I wish you had told me, we could have..." She trailed off.

"Thanks, Jakkie," Darius said. He was trying to say it loudly, but it was getting harder for him. Amelia sobbed, trying to get past Drake, but he held her firm Darius was dying and Carl just stood there, enjoying the show.

"You bastard!" Drake shouted, pivoting on the balls of his feet back to the shooter. His hands were fisted tight at his side and he shook with fury. "What kind of sicko are you to shoot someone in the back?"

"The dead kid is the son of a narc—"

"Shut up!" Jakkie shouted. "He's not dead yet!"

He just kept talking like she said nothing at all. "And that kid there," he used his gun to point at Andrew, "is a homo." He lifted the gun.

"Stop this! Stop!" Amelia screamed. Her voice sounded far away, foreign like it wasn't really her talking. Carl looked at her and smiled. It sent shivers down her spine. Lowering the rifle, Carl turned his full attention to her. "There you are," he said with a voice so cold it chilled her blood. "I should have expected you to be hiding behind someone else. You shouldn't have stuck your nose in my business."

"You killed someone!"

"Amelia," Drake snapped, shifting to block her more.

Carl raised the rifle, leveling it on them. Then suddenly shifted back to Andrew.

"No!" Drake shouted and lunged at Carl.

"Drake!" Amelia screamed.

Drake hit the floor.

More shots rang out, bullets pulverizing the cinderblock walls.

Chapter Twenty

AMELIA SCURRIED ACROSS THE FLOOR ON HER HANDS AND KNEES TO Drake, tears burning her eyes and blurring her vision. Cops were everywhere, climbing in through the windows, and rushing from the adjacent hallways. Carl and his backup turned to run but met the officers straight on. More shots and the three were on the floor. Amelia didn't care. Darius was dead, or just about, and Drake was shot.

"Drake," she whispered, her throat choking on her tears. She blinked and wiped her cheeks with the back of her hand. "Drake." All she could manage to say was his name.

Blood soaked his sleeve and he held it against his side. His face twisted into a pained grimace and he was breathing wrong, hard but shallow. Only the arm. *Oh thank you, God.* Amelia pressed her hand over the wound. Maybe if there were enough pressure the bleeding would stop. That was always what they did in movies, so there had to be some truth to it.

She wanted to stop the tears, but she couldn't. Drake yelled out in pain as she put pressure on it.

"I'm sorry," she whispered.

"No, not your fault," he said through clenched teeth. He reached across with his good arm and laid his hand over hers, helping her press on his wound.

"You're going to be okay," she said with as much courage and belief as she could muster, reaching down to the bottom of her soul. "Darius will be okay."

"I don't know about Darius," he said, his voice cracking.

Amelia looked down the hall to Jakkie and Darius. Jakkie's bloody hands covered her face and her body shook while she rocked back and forth on her knees. Darius was gone. Amelia looked back at Drake.

"He's reading Shakespeare under a tree with my mother," she choked out.

Drake nodded. He never let go of Amelia's hand.

A cop nearby snapped some orders to his officers and pointed toward the halls and windows. He spoke into his radio and nodded his head, making eye contact with Amelia. He looked furious.

"Where's Carl and the other guys?" Drake asked, slumping back in exhaustion. His grip on her hand loosened and slipped, but he didn't let go.

Amelia looked to the three bodies on the linoleum floor, blood spreading away from them. Police officers in bulletproof vests and riot gear stood over them, while others ran up and down the hall.

"I think they're dead," Amelia managed to force her throat to say.

Joaquin held Victoria as she wept, tears running down his own cheeks and Andrew sat against the wall with his arms resting on his raised knees, his head down. His shoulders shook.

Two officers ran down the hall, with EMTs immediately behind them. One EMT went to the three gunmen while the other crouched down, laying his fingers against Darius' throat. He scowled and shook his head, squeezing the radio on his shoulder.

Jakkie screamed and crumpled into a shaking heap.

"Over here," another officer said, motioning toward her and Drake. As the EMT with Darius stood, he shook his head at the officer. The officer opened his mic and said "Four more dead. Three appear to be the suspects. One student, another injured."

*More...*How many had died?

Four paramedics rounded the end of the hall, pulling two gurneys behind them. Two came straight to Drake. "You need to move, ma'am," one said, trying to push her away.

Sudden panic slammed her chest and she had to fight the urge to tell him no, she wouldn't leave him. Drake squeezed her hand and said her name, drawing her attention. "It's okay, Amelia."

She could only nod and fell backward, landing on her rump, scooting back to be out of their way as they took care of Drake. Jakkie's wailing made her turn, and she watched unable to react as Joaquin pulled Jakkie away from Darius' body and one of the paramedics covered him with a sheet. Andrew pushed up from the floor and walked to Amelia, crouching down beside her. A slow tremor worked its way through her, settling in her stomach, making her feel sick. She looked down at her hands, sticky with blood, red-black stains marring her pale yellow sweater.

"Oh, God..." she whispered.

"It's not your fault. I know you think it is, but it's not."

Amelia looked at him and raised her hands. "Would I have this blood on my hands if it wasn't my fault?"

"Yes, you would," Andrew said. He sat down next to her.

Amelia looked at the blood on her hands. She still felt guilty.

"You know, you most likely saved his life." Joaquin said, leading Jakkie and Victoria to Amelia and Andrew. "He was bleeding really badly and if you weren't militant about keeping pressure on it he could have bled to death before the EMTs got here."

Amelia rubbed her hands over her face, forgetting about the blood.

"Honey, if your Dad sees you with blood on your face he's going to freak out," Victoria said, her voice trembling as hard as Amelia's insides.

Amelia laughed, only because she didn't know what else to do. The laughter turned into more crying. She needed Da. She needed him so bad. On cue, Da's voice echoed down the hall, yelling her name.

"Amelia!"

Amelia scrambled to her feet, stumbling toward the sound of his voice.

"Get out of my way! My *daughter* is down there!"

The line of officers parted, and then Amelia was weeping in her father's embrace. He held on so tight she couldn't breathe, but she didn't care, didn't want to breathe. Didn't want to feel anything but Da's hug.

"Are you okay?" he asked against her hair, his accent so strong even she almost couldn't understand him. "Amelia…"

"It's not me that you need to worry about," she managed to say against his rough woolen jacket. "I'm fine."

"Amelia, you are my daughter. I will worry about you as much as I see fit." He pushed her away from him, looking her over. His eyes pinched when he saw her hands and sweater. "You have a lot of blood on you."

"It's not mine, Da. It's D-Drake's." Her voice broke when she said his name.

She bit her bottom lip. Saying it made it real. She knew it was real. There was *nothing* more *real* that watching someone get shot. But it was hazy, like she was running on auto pilot the whole time.

"He'll be fine. And you are fine," he said, firmly. His features wavered, his chin shaking. "It would have killed me if you got hurt." He ran his hand over her hair and kissed her forehead.

"Da, Darius is dead," she forced herself to say.

He looked her in the eyes. "What do you mean?"

"I mean he was shot and now he's dead."

The words tasted bitter.

"We'll get through that. One day at a time," he said and put his hand on her shoulder, squeezing gently.

Amelia nodded. "One day at a time. These days just keep getting harder and harder." She bit her bottom lip and let the tears run down her face. Her father pulled her to him again in a hard, desperate embrace.

In-person classes were cancelled until further notice, or until the kids could be shuffled off to other schools in the district and their high school could be cleaned up and repaired. Remote learning was the new norm.

Drake was admitted to the hospital, and even though she'd talked to him on the phone, she needed to go see him. She needed to talk to him, needed to see with her own eyes he was okay. Amelia called the hospital the second night he was there and lied to the nurse to get information. She said she was his older sister in college and wanted to see how he was doing. Apparently, he lost a lot of blood. The nurse said a brown-haired girl was found applying pressure to his wound and it saved his life. The bullet nicked an artery and broke his collarbone.

He was okay, but she almost lost him. She couldn't lose another person. She had already lost one that day.

Amelia had found out his room number when she called as his "sister," and snuck past the nurse's station to see him. With one last glance down the hall to make sure she was free and clear, she put on a happy face and walked in. No matter how much she thought she was ready, it hurt to see him. Physically hurt, right in the center of her chest. He looked like her mother had in the end. Needles Tend monitors and cords and the horrible hospital gown.

"Don't lie, I know you hate it," he said when she walked in.

"You caught me," she said as she walked over to the bed. "Can I sit down?"

"Please," he said, reaching out his good hand for her. Amelia sat on the edge of the bed, clear of the IV and cords.

Her dad was waiting downstairs. It was one thing for her to sneak in, but her dad would fail miserably as a spy. He knew it. She knew it. They just left it at that and he waited for her until she was ready to go.

"I needed to make sure you were okay." Amelia's voice cracked and she cleared her throat, looking down at their joined hands. "The nurse said…" She paused, unable to stop the tears running down her face. "The nurse said you lost a lot of blood."

"The nurse told me that, too. But the nurse also told me a paramedic told her about this girl with brown hair and gray eyes that stayed with me and applied pressure to my arm. And if this beautiful girl hadn't done that, I might not be here right now."

Her body shook, and tears choked her. She couldn't look him in the eyes.

"I can't lose you, Drake. You — you mean t-too much to me," she stuttered.

Drake shifted forward, leaning on his good arm so they were almost eye-to-eye and nose-to-nose. "Amelia, you are my best friend. More than Joaquin and Andrew and Darius combined." Drake paused and bit his bottom lip. He took her hand again. "Amelia, I love you."

"I love you, too." She didn't even pause to tell him the same, the words coming easily, and with the words a great lightness replaced the heavy sorrow in her chest.

She leaned forward and kissed him.

Chapter Twenty-One

There were the bad days and then there were the really bad days, where you just wanted to curl up into a little ball in a dark corner and hide from the rest of the world until it spun past you. Today was one of those really bad days.

The last time she had had one of those really bad days was her mother's funeral. Today was Darius' funeral. Her mother's death didn't make sense to her. Darius' death made her mad.

Amelia was in all black down to the elastic she had in her hair. Drake had a little bit harder time sticking with the black. The cast he had on his shoulder and arm was neon orange. He wanted to go with a more neutral color because he knew this was coming, but Amelia said if he was going to have plaster on him for the next six weeks he should have something he *wanted* to have. With that being said, he got neon orange. It only peeked out once in a while from underneath the long coat he wore draped over his shoulder.

It was an open casket. Since Darius had been shot in the back they could show his face. If Amelia didn't know any better she could have sworn he was breathing. It would be just like Darius to pull a prank like that. She'd sat between her father on one side and Drake and his parents on the other side through the wake, each of them holding one of her hands, with the others behind them — Jakkie, Victoria, Joaquin, and Andrew. Joaquin and Andrew sat on either side of Jakkie, holding her hands just like Da and Drake did for Amelia. Sometimes simple contact was the only thing that kept them grounded.

Christmas Eve was spent at the funeral home hearing what the minister and other speakers had to say. One by one they all started crying. Drake grabbed Amelia's hand and she cried on his non-plastered arm.

Amelia hated she was at a funeral on Christmas Eve, but apparently there was some meaning to his family having it on Christmas Eve. It was his favorite day of the year. Everyone in his family would gather around and just talk. And not about work, it would be about how things had changed this past year and how they were looking forward to the next year. It was a time of reflection and a time to be with family. His family believed he would want to be around on this day, so he was still a part of their lives. The thought made Amelia cry.

Again.

More....she never really stopped.

After the eulogy at the funeral home, everyone followed the black hearse to a cemetery across town where Darius' family had always been laid to rest. The air was crisp, and hard, biting Amelia's exposed skin. A sudden thaw in the last few days allowed the ground to soften enough for Darius' grave to be dug, otherwise they would have had to wait till spring and go through this all over again. Part of her was glad the torture would not be relived in just a few months.

Da stood on one side and Drake on the other, two pillars of strength on each side holding her hands just as they had through the service. Her breath curled in front of her face each time she exhaled, and her cheeks prickled with wind-chilled dampness.

"His dad is quitting his job. He knew he was putting his life on the line, but never considered his children could be in danger, too," Drake said, leaning over to speak close to her ear.

"Darius has siblings?" Amelia asked. Drake nodded.

"He has a little sister." He kind of pointed with his cast at the family staring at the hole in the ground as they lowered the casket. "She's five years old."

"Oh, God," Amelia whispered. "She mustn't understand what's going on."

Drake nodded. The preacher doing the ceremony stepped forward and spoke up.

"Darius was strong, and in the end, he was a hero. He acted without hesitation, without remorse, to protect his friends. In his last few breaths, he told the girl he loved that he loved her. I understand she told him she loved him back. Darius died happy. He died a hero. He died a true friend."

Somewhere in the crowd, Amelia heard Jakkie's weeping.

"We should all do what he did. Love to the end." The casket was lowered into the ground and one by one the people left. Amelia moved to walk away, turning her back on the hole in the ground. Drake walked with her, holding her hand.

"Out of all the cemeteries in the city, Darius had to be buried in this one," she said.

She looked over her shoulder, caught Da's attention, and waved at him. He waved back, his smile just a little strained, and went back to the people he was talking to. Parents and teachers from school. This wasn't the first funeral her father had attended in the last two days, and it wasn't the last. Six students had died in the shootings, another four were injured, and two teachers would be out of school the rest of the year as they recovered from their wounds.

Her pain was so raw; she knew each service had to rip Da apart a little bit, too. How could it not?

'What's so special about this one?" Drake asked. Amelia turned around, walking backward. She wanted to make eye contact with Drake.

"My mother is buried in this one."

Drake stopped short. "I had no idea. You really did grow up not far away."

"I know." She reached for his hand and he took it. She pulled him up to her. "I think it's time the two of you met."

They wandered around the cemetery. It was the largest one in the city so they had a bit of walking to do. The sky was cloud-covered but warmed up a bit. The grass was not frozen and the dirt was mud, but at least it was not snowing. It was nice to take a winter walk. So they just walked at a leisurely pace, holding hands and talking. It was all Amelia ever wanted. Nothing fancy or crazy, something she would always love.

"Here she is." Amelia smiled, stopping in front of a rose granite headstone. "My mother. Lily MacDonald."

She looked at Drake. He looked at the stone.

"How did she die?" he asked.

"Cancer of the heart muscle. It's really rare. She lasted three times longer than they gave her. She always liked to rub it in the doctor's face. She was stronger than they thought. But she had one bad day and she went downhill. She waited till my birthday before she was mentally gone. I thank her every day for that."

"You thank her?" Drake asked.

"Do you ever hear me talking but I'm not talking to anyone?"

Drake nodded. "Once in a while." He quirked a quick smile. "I just figured you were a little bit crazy." He winked. "Just a little...but I love that about you."

"I talk to my mother," she explained, ignoring his teasing. For now. "She helped me get through so much. The first day of school, the tagging, when I went to Weaver's office," she listed. "And other times."

Drake was silent, holding her hand a little tighter. Then he took a single step forward.

"Hi, Mrs. MacDonald. I'm Drake."

Amelia smiled.

"This is the Drake I've been telling you about, Mom. He's the best boyfriend ever, and I love him with all my heart."

Dear Mom,

I am writing to tell you what is going on with everything.

Drake and I have gotten really close and are now officially dating. I know you always said you wanted me to have someone good in my life, like Da, and he is. Mom, you would really approve of him. I know it. I mean, Da does...that should say it all.

We walk by Darius' grave once a week and talk to him just like we do you. I know you would appreciate us coming to see you and I know Darius loves to have company. The high school is going to dedicate the newly renovated courtyard to Darius and the other kids who died that day. There were eight in all, and another half dozen who were hurt. We had to be bused all over the city for a month or so, until they got the school workable again, and now we all live with the sound of construction all day. But, the governor stepped in and gave the school money to renovate, so maybe the school will come out better in the end.

We're graduating next week. Drake is the class valedictorian, no surprise there. What he never told me when he confessed the college he wanted to go to turned him down was that a bunch of other colleges had accepted him because of his grades. Don't worry, I've smacked him a bit for this, but he never accepted admission because he was so set on going to the New York School of Music. Some have offered him deferred admission, so he can go a year later than he should have, and some are offering him additional scholarship money for his music. Not a full ride, but it's more than they offered before. He's not slouching off for the year, though. He's going to take some classes locally and transfer them.

Funny thing is, when we were at the community campus checking out stuff he saw this flyer posted on a bulletin board about this small music institute right here in New York City. He'd never heard of them before, but they're a lot cheaper than any other place he's looked, and they'd give him what he wants. He's checking them out before he decides anything.

I'm so proud of him.

So college...did you like my segue there?

You know I always planned on going to the university Da taught at, but since Da's school closed down, everything changed. I hope you weren't angry with us for not telling you what happened before you left, and I know you understand. Anyway, I decided to go to the community college on the other side of town. I will still be living with Da. I know he likes that idea, and it'll help make things more manageable for a while. And I can transfer to a four-year school after two years. There's one a bit out of the city a friend of Drake's goes to. It's called Clarkmore.

It's not the way I'd planned, but nothing about the last year has been what I planned. I've learned the universe will figure it out; I just need to bend rather than break. Besides, I don't want to leave Da alone. He may try to look strong, but I know he misses you. We've into a better apartment in a secure, safe building and I got my own bedroom again. Yay! It's in a little better part of town, and we're going to take the bus to school in the morning.

Now when I say "we," I'm talking about the group: Jakkie, Victoria, Joaquin, Andrew, Drake, and I. We are all going to the community college, at least for now. Drake and

I managed to convince everyone they had choices, even if they didn't think they did.

But I still don't know what I want to do. I think maybe...maybe...I want to be a teacher, just like you and Da. Maybe.

I never understood how people my age could have their whole lives planned out. We are still so young. But that's what community college is for, right? Help us figure out what we want to do. That and get all the pre-req classes out of the way. Drake is the only one with any kind of clear idea, and beyond "Music," that's all he's got. But, music is in him.

I've considered learning how to play an instrument. How crazy is that?

I wanted to say happy birthday! I won't put down on paper how old you would be, but it was still your birthday today. This is the first birthday you aren't with us. It is hitting Da and me hard. We miss you, Mom. And we love you.

I know you won't read this letter, you won't need to because you're in my heart, but it helps me to put the words down on paper and I'm still going to leave it on your grave when Drake and I come by and see you today.

I love you.

Amelia

The End

About Katie Charles

Katie Charles lives in Kansas City with her family: husband Daniel, stepdaughter Katie, and biological daughter Maebh.

She has three dogs: Eloise a Chihuahua pug mix, Sasha a Boxer Mastiff mix, and Kenna a Cavalier King Charles Spaniel. They also have a cat, Kitters an orange tabby.

When not writing Katie can be found reading, crocheting, watching Blippi and Meekah, or teaching high school science at her day job.

See more at KatieCharles.com